MD

W9-CDI-724

RANDOM HOUSE

LARGE PRINT

JOHNNY ANGEL

Also by Danielle Steel
available from Random House Large Print

Dating Game
Answered Prayers
Sunset in St. Tropez
The Cottage
The House on Hope Street
Irresistible Forces
Journey
The Kiss
Leap of Faith
Lone Eagle
The Wedding

DANIELLE STEEL

JOHNNY ANGEL

RANDOM HOUSE
LARGE PRINT

This book is a work of fiction.
Names, characters, places and incidents are
either the product of the author's imagination
or are used fictitiously. Any resemblance to
actual persons, living or dead, events or
locales, is entirely coincidental.

Copyright © 2003 by Danielle Steel

All rights reserved under International and
Pan-American Copyright Conventions.
Published in the United States of America by
Random House Large Print in association
with Delacorte Press, New York and
simultaneously in Canada by Random House
of Canada Limited, Toronto.
Distributed by Random House, Inc.,
New York.

*The Library of Congress has established a
Cataloging-in-Publication record for this title.*

0–375–43207–8

www.randomlargeprint.com

FIRST LARGE PRINT EDITION

10 9 8 7 6 5 4 3 2 1

This Large Print edition published in accord
with the standards of the N.A.V.H.

To Nicky angel,
I will always love you,
and you will always be
with me, in my heart.
                    Mom.

And to Julie,
  who was Nicky's angel,
and mine.

I know that they are
together now, happy,
laughing, full of love
and mischief.
How very, very much
we will miss you both
until we meet again.
                    with all my love,
                        d.s.

JOHNNY ANGEL

Athens Regional Library
2025 Baxter Street
Athens, GA 30606

Chapter One

The sun was shining brightly on a hot June day in San Dimas, a somewhat distant suburb of L.A. The sophistication of Los Angeles and Hollywood seemed light-years from here. The city was just far enough so as to seem not to exist at all, and kids could still be kids on a warm summer day. School was drawing to a close before summer vacation, graduation was about to fall like a ripe plum into the seniors' hands, and the prom was only days away.

Johnny Peterson was the valedictorian of the senior class, and the star of both the track and the football teams for the past four years. He and Becky Adams had been going out for four years. They were standing on the school steps, talking to a group of friends, his tall lanky body swaying ever so slightly in her direction, as their eyes met from time to time. They shared the same barely guarded secret that many of the kids their age did. They were in love with each other, had been sleeping with each other for the past year, and had been seeing each other exclusively before that for all of their high school years. High school sweethearts, with vague but unspoken plans to wind up together one day. Johnny was about to turn eighteen in July, before starting college. Becky had turned eighteen in May.

His dark brown hair shone in the summer sunshine, with copper lights that seemed to be reflected in his dark brown eyes. He was tall, broadshouldered, and athletic, had great teeth and a perfect smile. He looked the way every young man wished he could as a high school senior, but few do. But more than that, he was a terrific kid, and a nice guy. He had always been a good student, had lots of friends, and had two jobs when he wasn't playing sports and on weekends. His parents had very little money with three kids to support, and often just managed to get by. But they always did. He would have liked to play pro football and could have, but he had very sensibly decided to go to state college on a scholarship, and study accounting, so he could help his dad. His dad ran a small accounting firm, and had never much liked what he did. But Johnny didn't seem to mind it, and was a whiz in math. And his excellent computer skills were a huge help too. His mom had been a nurse and had retired years before, to take care of his younger brother and sister, which had turned out to be a full-time job, especially in the past five years. Charlotte, his little sister, had just turned fourteen and was starting high school in the fall. And Bobby, who was nine, was a special child.

Becky's family was not as orderly as

Johnny's. She had four brothers and sisters, and their life had pretty much fallen apart two years before, when her dad died. He was a construction worker, and was killed in a freak accident. It left the family financially desperate and stunned. Becky had two jobs after school, and worked hard. They needed every penny she and her oldest brother could earn. And unlike Johnny, her scholarship hadn't come through. She was going to work full time at the drugstore all year, and try again for a scholarship next year. And she didn't really mind. She wasn't the student Johnny was, and she was relieved to have a break from school. She liked working, loved her two sisters and two brothers, and was happy to help her mom in whatever way she could. They had gotten pitifully little money from her dad's insurance, and things had been tough for a long time. Johnny was the sweet spot in her life.

Her hair was as fair as his was dark,

her eyes as blue as the summer sky. She was a pretty girl, and she loved him.

She worried a little about his going to college and meeting other girls, but she knew he loved her. Everyone in their class said they were the perfect couple, they were always together, always laughing, talking, joking, happy, and they never seemed to fight. As much as they were boyfriend and girlfriend, they were also best friends. And because of that, Becky had fewer friends than she might have otherwise. She and Johnny spent every minute together they could. They went to class together, and saw each other at night, whenever possible, after sports, homework, and jobs. And they were both so conscientious, their parents no longer complained about how much they saw each other. They were rarely apart.

And as they stood at the center of a cluster of high school seniors, everyone was talking about graduation and prom. They had kept it a secret between them, but Johnny had paid for her dress. Without his help, she couldn't have gone. And she smiled up at him now, four years of love and confidences and secrets between them, and her eyes seemed to light up like fireworks when she looked at him.

"I've got to get going, you guys. I have to get to work," Johnny said, smiling at his friends. He worked at a nearby lumber company, taking inventory, sorting stock, and sawing wood. And he made good money for hard work. Becky was already working at the drugstore job that was about to become full time for her, and had just given up her second job waitressing in a coffee shop near school. It was going to be a lot easier for her now working in just one place. Johnny worked for his father on weekends, and the lumber supply company after practice and games. He was going to work for them full time all summer, to make as much money as he could before school. "Come on, Becky," he tugged at her arm, to pull her away from the girls who were still talking about what they were wearing to the prom that was two days away. For most of them, it was the end of an era, the culmination of a dream. And it was for Becky and Johnny too. But they had had none of the stress and panic of some of the others, wondering who to take as their dates. Their relationship gave them both confidence, and an unusual amount of emotional support. High school had been easier for them because of that.

Becky finally managed to tear herself away from their friends, and tossed her long blond hair over her shoulder as she followed Johnny to his car. He was carrying both their backpacks, and threw them easily into the backseat as he glanced at his watch. "Do you want to pick up the kids?" He tried to do that with her as often as he could. He was one of those people who enjoyed helping people out, and often did.

"Do you have time?" she asked comfortably. In some ways, they already seemed married, and in their heart of hearts they knew that they would be one day. It was another of the unspoken secrets they shared. They were so close, had grown up together, and sometimes it seemed like they didn't even need words.

"Sure, I've got time," he smiled at her, as she slid into her seat, and turned on the radio. They liked the same music, the same people, the same food. She loved watching him play football, he loved dancing with her, and talking to her for hours on the phone, after work. Most nights, he dropped by her house on his way home. And then he'd call her when he finished his homework. His mother said they were like Siamese twins.

The school where her younger siblings went was only four blocks away, and all four of them were hanging out in the schoolyard when they got there and Becky waved. The four Adams kids came thundering toward them, and as Becky leaned forward to let them in, they piled unceremoniously into the back of the car.

"Hi, Johnny," both boys said in unison, and Peter, the oldest one, at twelve, thanked him for the ride. They were nice, wholesome kids. Mark was eleven, Rachel was ten, and Sandi was seven. Theirs was a noisy, loving, lively house, and two years after he had died, they all still missed their dad. All their mom had done in the past two years was chase after them, and work too hard. She looked ten years older than she had when Mike had died. And although her friends kept telling her she should start dating, she just looked at them as though they were crazy, and told them she had no time. But it was more than that, and Becky knew it. Her mom had never loved anyone except her dad, and couldn't bear the thought of going out with another man. They had been high school sweethearts too.

Johnny dropped off Becky and the kids, she kissed him lightly before she got out, and he waved at all of them as he drove away. And as he disappeared down the street at full speed, she shepherded the others into the house, and helped them to get snacks and drinks, before leaving for work. She knew her mom would be home from her job in two hours. She ran the local beauty school. She was a pretty woman, life just hadn't turned out the way she'd dreamed. She had never expected to wind up alone at forty, with five kids.

Johnny was back at Becky's front door again four hours later, looking tired and happy. He stayed long enough to eat a sandwich with her at the kitchen table, chat with her mom, tease the kids, and head home by nine-thirty. His days were long and full.

"I can't believe it's almost graduation, seems like just last year you two were about five years old and going trick-or-treating together." Pam Adams shook her head and smiled as she watched Johnny unwind his long frame from the kitchen chair. He had played basketball in his freshman year, and been good at it, but eventually football and track had taken up all his time. Pam looked at Johnny gratefully, he was such a nice kid. She hoped he and Becky would get married one day, and that he would live a longer life than her husband had. But the years she'd shared with Mike had been so very good, she didn't regret an instant of them, just the fact that he was gone. "Thank you for getting Becky's dress for her," she said softly. She was the only one who knew. He hadn't even told his mom and dad.

"It looks great on her," Johnny said easily, slightly embarrassed by the look of gratitude in her mother's eyes. "We'll have a good time." He had ordered a corsage for her too.

"I hope so. Becky's dad and I got engaged at senior prom." She said it nostalgically, but it wasn't a hint to him. It was pretty obvious that they were heading that way too, with or without a ring.

"See you tomorrow," Johnny said as he left, and Becky followed him outside.

They stood next to his car for a few minutes, chatting, and he took her in his arms and they kissed. It was a kiss filled with passion, emotion, all the feelings they shared, and the energy of youth, and she was breathless when they stopped.

"You'd better go before I drag you into the bushes, Johnny Peterson," she said with a giggle, and the smile that still tore his heart out after all these years.

"That sounds pretty good. Your mom might get a little upset," he teased. None of their parents knew, or so they thought, how far things had gone, although unbeknownst to them, both their mothers were well aware of it. Pam had had a talk with Becky once, and urged her to be careful. But they both were. They were both sensible kids and, so far at least, had had no slip-ups and no scares. Becky had no intention of getting pregnant before they got married, and that was still years away. Johnny had to finish school, and so did she, and she wasn't even starting for another year. They were in no hurry, they had all the time in the world. "I'll call you later," he promised, as he got into his car. He knew his mother would be waiting for him, most likely with something to eat, even though he'd eaten at Becky's house. And with no homework to do, he might spend some time with the kids and his dad. Depending on how things were when he got home.

He lived only two miles from Becky's house, and he was home five minutes later. He parked in the driveway behind his dad's car, and as he walked through the backyard he saw his younger sister Charlotte shooting baskets by herself, the way he used to do. She looked just like their mother, and a little like Becky, with big blue eyes and long blond hair. She was wearing shorts and a tank top, and her legs were nearly as long as his. She was tall for her age, and beautiful, but she didn't really care. The only thing that interested Charlotte was sports. She ate, slept, dreamed, and talked about nothing but baseball in the summer, football and basketball in the winter, and she played on every team she could. She was the most perfect all-around athlete, male or female, Johnny had ever known.

"Hi Charlie, how's it going?" he said, as he caught the ball she tossed at him. It always made him smile because she threw like a guy. She had a remarkable talent for sports.

"Okay," she glanced over her shoulder at him after he threw the ball back to her, and she sank another basket. And he could see, when she looked at him, that her eyes were sad.

"What's up?" He put an arm around her, and she stopped for a minute, and leaned against him. He could feel the sadness emanating through her. In the last few years, she seemed older than she was, in part because she was tall. But she was also wise beyond her years.

"Nothing."

"Is Dad home?" But he knew he was, by the car. Johnny knew what was bothering her. It wasn't new to either of them, but it still hurt, after all these years.

"Yeah." She nodded, and then started to dribble the ball, as Johnny watched her for a minute, and then grabbed the ball from her. They played together for a few minutes, taking turns sinking baskets, and it struck him again how good she was. It was a shame in some ways that she wasn't a boy. And he knew she thought so too. She had gone to almost every game he'd played through all his high school years, and rooted passionately for him. Johnny was exactly who she wished she could be. He was her hero, more than anyone on earth.

It was a full ten minutes later when he finally left her, and went inside. His mother was standing in the kitchen, drying dishes, while his little brother Bobby watched her from the kitchen table, and his father was in the living room, watching TV.

"Hi, Mom," he said, planting a kiss somewhere on the top of her head, as she smiled. Alice Peterson was crazy about her kids, and always had been. The happiest day in her life was when Johnny was born. And she still felt that way when she looked at him now.

"Hi, sweetheart, how was your day?" Her eyes lit up when she saw him, as they did every night. She had always had a special bond with him.

"Pretty good. Graduation's on Monday, and the prom is in two days." She laughed at what he said, as Bobby watched.

"No kidding. Did you think I forgot? How's Becky?" Both kids had talked of nothing else for months.

"Good." And then he turned his attention to Bobby, who smiled as his big brother approached. "Hi, kiddo, good day?" Bobby said nothing, but the smile broadened as Johnny tousled his hair.

Johnny had long-running conversations with him, told him everything he did every day, and inquired about his little brother's day. But Bobby never spoke, hadn't in five years, since he was four. He had had an accident with his father, when their father drove his car off a bridge into the river. They had both nearly drowned, and a passerby had saved Bobby's life. He had been on life support for two weeks, and he had survived it, but he never spoke again. No one had been able to figure out since then if it was brain damage from being submerged for too long, or trauma. But no amount of specialists, therapy, or treatments had changed anything. Bobby was alert, aware, and carefully observed everything around him, but he did not speak. He was in a special school for the handicapped, and he participated in some things, but he lived in a world that was airtight now, and completely sealed. He could write, but never communicated in writing either. He just copied the words and letters other people wrote. He did not answer questions, verbally or in writing. He did not volunteer anything. It was as though Bobby had nothing left to say. And ever since the accident, what had once been a tendency for their father to drink a little too much at parties had become a nightly anesthesia, so he wouldn't have to think. He never fell down, he never got sloppy, he wasn't aggressive or violent. He just sat down in front of the TV and got quietly drunk every night, and it was no mystery why. It was just the way things were, and had been for five years.

None of them ever spoke about it. Alice had tried talking to him about it at first, and she had thought he'd get over it, just as Bobby would get over his silence. But neither of them had. And in their own way, they were both locked into their own worlds. Bobby into his silent bubble, and Jim into his beer. It was hard on all of them, but they all understood by now, and accepted, that it wasn't going to change. She had suggested AA to him several times, and he just brushed her off. He refused to discuss his drinking with her or anyone else. He didn't even acknowledge that he drank.

"Are you hungry, sweetheart?" his

mom asked him. "I saved dinner for you."

"I'm okay. I had a sandwich at the Adamses'," he said, gently touching Bobby's cheek. Touching him seemed like the best way of communicating with him sometimes, and Johnny felt closer than ever to him. They had a bond that was unbreakable, and Bobby just followed him around sometimes, in his familiar silence, with huge, loving blue eyes.

"I wish you'd wait and eat here once in a while," his mother said. "How about dessert? We had apple pie." It was his favorite, and she made it for him as often as she could.

"That sounds good." He didn't want to hurt her feelings. Sometimes he ate two full dinners, one at Becky's house, and one at home, just to please her. Johnny was crazy about her, and she about him. They were more than just mother and son. They were friends.

She sat down at the kitchen table with him while he ate his pie, and Bobby watched him. Johnny and his mom chatted about what was going on, Charlotte's home runs that afternoon, and the prom. He was going to pick up his rented tux the next day. She could hardly wait to see him in it, and had bought some film that day so she could take his picture, and she offered to buy Becky a corsage.

"I already ordered one," he smiled at his mother, "but thanks anyway." And then he said he had to work on his graduation speech. As valedictorian, he had to make the opening speech. And she was unreservedly proud of him, as she had been all his life.

He stopped in the living room for a minute on his way upstairs. The TV was blaring, and his father was sound asleep. It was a familiar scene. Johnny turned off the television, and went quietly upstairs, sat down at his desk, and looked at what he'd already written. He was still poring over it, when the door to his room opened and closed silently, and he saw Bobby sit down on his bed.

"I'm working on a speech," Johnny explained, "for graduation. It's in four days." Bobby said nothing, and Johnny went back to his work. He was comfortable with Bobby just sitting in his room, and Bobby seemed happy to be there. Eventually, Bobby lay down on the bed, and stared up at the ceiling. At times like that, it was hard not to wonder what was on his mind, if he still remembered the accident and thought about it. If his not speaking had been a decision, or something he couldn't help. There was no way to know.

The accident had taken a toll on all of them in the past five years. In some ways, they all worked harder, like he and Charlotte, to be even more than they might have been otherwise, to make up for the grief they had all shared. And in other ways, they had given up, like their father, who hated his job, hated his life, drank himself into a stupor every night, and was consumed with guilt. And Johnny knew that in her own way, their mother had given up too. She had given up the hope of Bobby ever speaking again, or Jim forgiving himself for what he'd done. She had never gotten angry at him, never accused him of being careless. He had had a few beers under his belt when he drove off the bridge. But she didn't have to accuse him of anything. Jim Peterson hated himself for what he'd done. It was one of those tragedies that could not be reversed. But they had all lived past it, they had gone on. Things were different than they had been, always would be now. It was just the way things were.

Johnny worked on his speech for another half-hour, and seemed satisfied with what he'd done, when he went to lie down next to Bobby on the bed. The child lay peacefully beside him, in silence, as Johnny held his hand. It was as though the words he wanted to share with him, and the feelings, passed through their fingers. What they felt for each other transcended words and sounds. They didn't need to say any-thing.

They lay that way for a long time, until their mother came upstairs to find Bobby, and told him he had to go to bed. He didn't nod, and his eyes said nothing at all, but he got up slowly, and looked at Johnny, and then walked qui-etly back to his own room, as his mother followed to put him to bed. She hadn't left him for a single day since the accident. She was always there for him. She never left him with sitters, never went anywhere. Her whole life re-volved around him. And the others un-derstood. It was her gift to him.

It was eleven o'clock when Johnny finally called Becky, and she answered the phone on the second ring. Her mother and the other kids had already gone to bed, but she always waited up for Johnny's call, and he never failed to call her. They liked talking to each other at day's end. And every morning, he picked her and the other kids up on the

way to school. His days began and
ended with her.

"Hi, baby. How's it going?" He
smiled whenever he spoke to her.

"Okay. Mom's in bed. I was just looking at my dress." He could hear the
smile in her voice, and it made him
happy for her. It was a beautiful dress,
and she looked fantastic in it. She was a
spectacular-looking girl, and he felt
lucky that she was his.

"You're going to be the prettiest girl
there," he said, and meant every word
of it.

"Thanks. How are things at your
house?" She worried about him, she
knew about the problem with his father.
Everyone did. He had been drinking for
years. And she felt sorry for Bobby
too. He was such a cute kid. She liked
Charlotte too, she was such a tomboy,
but she was a lot like Johnny. She was
really smart, and very kind, like their
mom. It was a lot harder to get to know
their dad.

"Same as always. Dad's passed out in

front of the TV, and Charlie looks kind of sad. She always wants him to come to her games, and he never does. Mom said she hit two home runs today, but it's like it doesn't matter to her unless Dad knows. He always used to come to my games, but I guess he thinks it's not the same with girls. People can be so dumb sometimes." It made him sad that he couldn't change it for her. He had tried talking to his father about it, but it was as though he didn't hear or care. So Johnny usually went to Charlie's games when he could. "I finished my speech. I hope it goes okay."

"It'll be great, you know that. I'm going to be so proud of you," she said, and meant it. They gave each other the support and comfort they each needed, and that their parents no longer had time for. There had been enough sorrow in both houses to keep both their mothers busy and distracted. It was part of the bond that cemented Becky and Johnny to each other. In some ways, they each were all they had, despite brothers and sisters and parents, and friends. They gave each other something no one else did.

"I'll see you tomorrow, sweetheart." There was nothing much to say, they just liked to hear each other's voice before they went to bed.

"I love you, Johnny," she said softly, sitting at the kitchen phone in her nightgown, thinking of him.

"I love you too, baby. Sleep tight." They hung up, and Johnny walked slowly up the stairs to his room in the silent house.

Chapter Two

"*Wow! You look gorgeous!*" Alice Peterson beamed at her elder son as he came down the stairs from his bedroom in his rented tux. He looked tall and dark and handsome, in a pleated white shirt, a dinner jacket that fit him exceptionally well, and he had a white rose pinned to his lapel. "You look like a movie star," and although she didn't say it to him, he looked like he was getting married. He was a strikingly handsome young man.

He went to take his corsage of white roses for Becky out of the refrigerator, and stood in the hall holding the clear plastic box, as Charlotte bounced down the stairs and stopped with a wide grin

on her face. As usual, she had a basketball in her hands.

"How do you think your brother
looks?" their mother asked with a look
of pride, as her daughter guffawed.

"Like a dork," she said unceremoniously, and Johnny laughed.

"Thanks, sis. You'll look just as dorky
one of these days when you go to the
senior prom. I can't wait! You'll probably take a basketball with you, or wear
your baseball mitt. You might even go
in cleats if nothing's changed by then."

"Yeah, I might," she grinned broadly
at him, and then conceded sheepishly, "I
guess you look okay." And like her
mother, she looked proud of him.

"He looks a lot better than okay,"
their mother said, standing on tiptoe to
give him a kiss, as Bobby wandered in
from the kitchen and stared. Their
mother snapped two quick pictures of
Johnny before he could object.

"How do I look to you, champ?"
Johnny addressed him without waiting
for a response, as Bobby watched the

scene with interest. Their father hadn't come home yet. "I'd better go pick Becky up, or we'll be late," he said, walking toward the door as his mother and sister watched him admiringly, and he turned to give them a last wave. And a moment later, they heard him drive away.

Becky was waiting for him on her front porch, in the white satin strapless dress he'd bought for her. It molded her figure perfectly, without being too tight, and she looked like a fairy princess, one of her sisters had said. She was wearing her long blond hair in a French twist, and the pair of white satin high-heeled pumps she had bought herself. Johnny pinned the white rose corsage on her, and she smiled up at him adoringly. He bent to kiss her then, and her brothers, standing nearby, hooted and jeered, as her mother came out from the kitchen to smile at them.

"You both look like you belong in a magazine," Pam Adams said with a loving grin. Becky looked prettier than ever that night, and Johnny looked more than his nearly eighteen years. "Have a good time, kids. This is your one and only senior prom. One day it'll be an important memory . . . enjoy every minute of it, and make it a night you'll never forget." Every moment seemed precious to her now. She had learned irrevocably that in the end, memories were all you had.

"We will, Mom," Becky said, and kissed her on the cheek as she left.

"Drive carefully," she admonished them, and Johnny promised her that he would, as he always did. He was sensible and responsible, and she had never worried about him, it was just something she said.

They met half a dozen of their friends at a nearby restaurant, everyone was in great spirits, and all the girls admired each other's dresses. They were all wearing corsages like hers, and the boys were all wearing roses on their lapels. They looked young and happy and excited, and when they left for the prom at eight-fifteen, they were all in a good mood. One of the other couples had decided to ride with them, having gotten a ride to the restaurant with someone else. And by nine o'clock they were at the dance.

It was a fun night for all of them. There was a live band, for most of the night, and one of the seniors acted as deejay between sets. The music was good, the food was plentiful, and only a few of their friends sneaked in booze and beer. Most of the students were content to stay sober for the night. It was an exciting night for everyone, the usual romances seemed to thrive, there were a few minor arguments, and only one fight broke out between two troublemakers, but it was quickly squelched. It was a night without mishap or event, and at midnight, when the dance ended, everyone stood outside, deciding where to go next. There was an all-night diner nearby where they all liked to go for

hamburgers, and some of the boys decided to go to a local bar and try out
their fake IDs.

Johnny and Becky had danced most
of the night, talked to friends, said hello
to almost everyone, and by the end of
the night, they were ready to go to Joe's
Diner for hamburgers and shakes, with a
large group of their friends. They offered a ride to the same couple that had
come with them, and at twelve-thirty
they were driving away from the
school, when a car full of guys from the
football team sped by in a convertible
and blew kisses at the girls. They
honked their horn frantically, and
shouted at Johnny, asking if he wanted
to race, and he shook his head with a
grin. He didn't like playing games like
that, particularly on a night like tonight,
and with two girls in the car. And as he
honked his horn good-naturedly at
them, they flew by in the convertible,
and careened off at the next intersection, heading for the only bar in town
that turned a blind eye to serving kids.

Becky and the other girl were talking and laughing, and gossiping about their friends, when they reached the next intersection, and Johnny drove sedately into it when the light changed. He was telling the boy in the backseat a story about one of the guys on the football team when he saw something flash out of the corner of his eye, and heard a sudden blaring of horns and screeching of tires, and as he looked toward it, he saw the same convertible heading toward him, coming back the way they had come only a few minutes before. They were going nearly eighty miles an hour, and screaming wildly as they roared past the other cars, and Johnny stepped hard on the brake. But he suddenly realized, as he did, that he couldn't stop in time, and he turned sharply to avoid the speeding car, heading into the traffic coming the other way as Becky screamed.

What happened after that was a blur for all of them. There was a sudden crash, and a huge impact followed by an explosion of glass and the sound of grinding steel. One of the girls said later that it felt like they'd hit a wall. They were instantly surrounded by honking, spinning, veering cars, as the convertible stopped in the midst of the melee. The boys in it flew high and wide, only the driver was left in the car, as the others landed on top of other cars and on the street, and Johnny's car spun like a top. He had done everything he could to stop it, and it only came to rest finally pinned between the divider and a passing truck, and when it stopped, there was silence everywhere. A witness said later that Becky's dress was covered with blood, the windshield looked like crumpled cellophane, and there was soft moaning from the backseat. Becky was unconscious, and Johnny's head was bent over the steering wheel.

They had all had their seatbelts on, and there was no sound for what seemed like an eternity, until finally a man with a flashlight came and peered into the car, and as he shone the light on them, he could hear crying from the backseat. He could hear the sound of ambulances in the distance by then, and he was afraid to touch anyone. He just backed away, as he watched people slowly climbing out of cars, there were already half a dozen people sitting by the side of the road, looking bloodstained and dazed. Five cars and a truck had been involved in the accident, and someone said the truck driver was dead, but as the paramedics got out of the ambulance, he couldn't tell them much else.

"There are a bunch of kids hurt in the car over there," he said, pointing at Johnny's car, "but I heard someone cry . . . I think they're okay," he said, as he got back in his car, and the paramedics hurried toward Johnny's car as two more ambulances arrived on the scene with a fire rescue team. Soon there were flashing lights and paramedics everywhere, checking cars, applying bandages, helping people out of cars. Within minutes, there were four bodies lying on the side of the road with tarps on them, among them the truck driver, as one of the paramedics helped Becky out of the front seat of the car, looking dazed with a gash on the side of her face that was still dripping blood on her dress, and another paramedic gently moved Johnny away from the steering wheel and felt for a pulse, and the couple in the backseat got out on Becky's side, they were both shaken up but appeared to be unhurt. The paramedic shone a light into Johnny's eyes as the other three were led away, and then he felt for a pulse again. He looked into the face of the handsome boy in the tux, there was a huge bump on his head, and he knew instantly that he had broken his neck as he laid his head gently back against the seat, and signaled to one of the firemen, who rushed over to help.

"The kid in the driver's seat is dead," he said quietly, so the others wouldn't hear, and then he signaled for a gurney to come and take him away. They slipped him out of the car, and covered him, and Becky turned just as they were taking him away.

"What are you doing? Why are you doing that?" she screamed at them. "Take that thing off his face!" She ran toward them, still dripping blood everywhere in her ruined dress. The whole top of it was now red. And she ran toward Johnny's lifeless form and tried to grab at the tarp covering him, but one of the paramedics pulled her away. She fought him valiantly as he held her in his arms, and she sobbed.

"Come on over here," he said quietly, "you're all right . . . come and sit down. . . . We have to take you to the hospital," he said, holding her firmly by the arms, but she was hysterical. She was sobbing and clawing at him, and trying desperately to get away. "I have to go to Johnny . . . I have to . . . I have to . . ." She was gasping for air, and choking on sobs, as one of the firemen comforted her and held her in his arms. "That's Johnny . . . he can't be . . . he can't . . . oh God . . . no . . ." She sank slowly toward the pavement again, and the fireman picked her up easily and deposited her in an ambulance, and a moment later, they sped away.

It took two hours to clear the scene, get everyone to nearby emergency rooms, or on their way home. Parents were called, kids were given rides by police officers, and all five of the bodies were sent to the morgue. And three police officers and a highway patrolman divided up the list of addresses where they had to go, to break the news. The truck driver was from out of state, and all they had to do was notify the trucking firm, and they would take care of the rest.

The officer who went to Johnny's address knew who he was, and had a daughter in Charlotte's class. He had done painful tasks like this before, and he was dreading what he would see on the boy's mother's face. He knew what a great kid Johnny was. He rang the bell at three A.M., and he had to ring it again. Jim Peterson finally came to the door, in his pajamas, and Alice was standing behind him in an old dressing gown. They looked frightened as soon as they saw a policeman at the door.

"Is something wrong, Officer?" They had never had a problem with Johnny, and it seemed hard to imagine that he had been arrested now. They wondered if he'd been caught speeding, or had been arrested for being drunk. But any of those possibilities seemed impossible to believe.

"I'm afraid so," he said, addressing them both. "May I come in?" he asked cautiously as they stood aside, and he walked in to their living room, and stood there looking grim. "There's been an accident," he said as Alice caught her breath, and her hand went instinctively to Jim's arm and grabbed at him. "Your son John has been killed. I'm sorry, ma'am . . . Mr. Peterson . . . it was a six-vehicle collision, and there were a number of fatalities, I'm just so sorry that one of them was your son."

"Oh my God . . ." Alice said, feeling a

rush of panic wash over her like a tidal wave, still trying to sort out the words, "oh my God . . . no . . . that can't be . . . are you sure there isn't some mistake?" Jim hadn't said a word so far, but there were tears running down his face.

"Another car hit them and forced them between the divider and a truck. I don't think there was anything your son could have done to avoid the accident. It's a terrible thing when we lose young people like that. I know how you must feel." Alice wanted to say that there was no way he could know, but she couldn't speak. Her mind was whirling incoherently, and she felt faint, as the officer helped her to a seat. "Would you like a glass of water, ma'am?" She shook her head silently as tears streamed down her face.

"Where is he now?" she finally managed to croak out, thinking of him lying by the side of the road somewhere, or in his car. She wanted to hold him in her arms, or die with him. She couldn't even think.

"They've taken him to the county coroner. You'll have to make arrangements for him, and we'll do anything we can to help." She nodded again, as Jim Peterson walked into the kitchen on shaky legs and came back with a drink. It looked like water, but it was straight gin, and Alice knew from the look of terror in his eyes what it was. He looked panic-stricken, which was how she felt.

The officer stayed with them for another half-hour, and then left them, after telling them again how sorry he was. It was after four in the morning by then, and Alice and Jim sat in their living room, staring at each other, not knowing what to say or do. He took her in his arms finally, and they sat side by side on the couch and sobbed. They sat there that way for hours, and she didn't say anything to him when he went and got another drink. She almost wished she could find solace in that too. There was nothing to comfort her, to soften the blow, and when the sun came up, she felt as though the end of the world had come. It seemed particularly offensive that it was another brilliantly sunny day. She couldn't imagine a world without Johnny in it, a life that didn't include him. Hours before, he had walked out of the house in his tux, with a rose on his lapel, and now he was gone. It was a lie, she told herself, it had to be, a cruel prank someone had played on them, and any minute, he would walk in the door and laugh at them. The officer had told them, when they inquired, that Becky had escaped with only a gash on her cheek, and the other couple in the car had been unhurt. Johnny had taken the full brunt of it, and an evil fate had taken him from them. They were relieved to know that the others were all right, but it seemed so unfair that Johnny had been killed, and through no fault of his own. He hadn't been careless or irresponsible, hadn't been drunk, had done nothing to deserve what had happened to him. He had been the perfect boy, the perfect son, everyone's hero and friend, and now he was gone, at seventeen.

Pam Adams called them at seven o'clock, and they were still sitting in the living room. And by then, Jim had had enough gin to slur his words. Alice Peterson answered the phone, and burst into tears the minute she heard Pam's voice.

"Oh my God, Alice, I'm so sorry," Pam was crying too. She had brought Becky home from the hospital by then, and mercifully, they had sedated her when a plastic surgeon sewed up her face. He had said there would be no scar, not visibly at least, but she was still crying uncontrollably about their taking Johnny away. She refused to believe that he was dead. "I feel so terrible for all of you . . . what can I do for you?" She remembered what it had been like for her when Mike had been killed. It was unthinkable, unbearable, a shock and grief too great to bear, and somehow she imagined it had to be even worse for them now, with a son. "Can I come over and help with the kids?"

"I don't know," Alice said, sounding confused. It was impossible to absorb what had just happened to them, and she still had to tell the other children that Johnny was dead. It was unthinkable. She couldn't even imagine saying the words.

"Let me come over. I can be there in a few minutes," Pam said insistently. She knew how important it was at a time like this, to be surrounded by friends. And there would be so much to decide and to do. They would have to get him to a funeral home, select a casket and a room, pick out his clothes, tell the kids, write an obituary, arrange for visiting hours at the funeral home, and work out all the details for the funeral at their church, buy a plot in a cemetery and arrange for burial, all the while trying to deal with their own sense of shock and grief. Pam knew better than anyone how unbearable it was, and she wanted to do anything she could to help. And she was worried about Becky too. This was going to be intolerably hard for her. An impossible grief to bear at any age.

Pam appeared at their front door twenty minutes later, and sat with her arms around Alice for a while, while Jim went to dress. Pam put a pot of coffee on, and an hour later, as the two women sat in the kitchen, crying and blowing their noses, Charlotte wandered downstairs in shorts and tank top, with tousled hair.

"Hi, Mom," she said sleepily. She looked at both women, crying, and holding each other's hands, and it was easy to see that something terrible had happened, as fear crossed Charlotte's face like an express train. "What's wrong?"

Her mother looked at her with agony in her eyes, and without saying a word, she walked across the kitchen and put her arms around her.

"Mom, what is it? What happened?"

It was an instant in her life when she knew with absolute certainty that everything she knew and loved and counted on was about to change.

"It's Johnny . . . he had an accident . . . he was killed leaving the prom," her mother said, choking on the words, and Charlotte let out a long, agonized sound, a wail of pain, as she heard the words.

"No . . . no . . . Mom . . . noo . . . please. . . ." They clung to each other and sobbed, as Pam cried quietly, watching them, wanting to be there for them, but not wanting to intrude. And a few minutes later, Jim walked in, he had sobered up again, and all Alice could see was the devastation on his face. They all sat and cried together for a long time, and finally Alice went up to Bobby's room. He was awake and lying in bed, as he did sometimes, but she had a feeling that today he had sensed something was wrong, and he was hiding from it. Even his silence was not enough to shield him from the horror of this.

"I have something very sad to tell you," his mother said, pulling him into her arms to hold him, as she sat on his bed. "Johnny has gone away . . . to be in Heaven, with God. . . . He loved you very much, sweetheart," she said, sobbing as she held the child, and she could feel him shudder and then stiffen in her arms, but he said not a word. And when she pulled away to look at him, she could see that he was crying, soundlessly, agonized, as broken as the rest of them. The brother he had adored had been taken from them. He understood it perfectly, and he never stopped crying as Alice helped him dress. They went back downstairs hand in hand, and the rest of the day was a blur of pain.

Pam stayed with Bobby and Charlotte, while Jim and Alice went to the coroner's, and Alice gave a wail of grief as she saw her son, and held him in her arms. Jim had to pull her away from him finally. And they went to the funeral home to make arrangements after that. It was after lunchtime by the time they came home. Pam had quietly made lunch for all of them. Charlotte was sitting silently in the backyard, and Bobby was upstairs in his room.

It was on the news that afternoon, and people started calling and dropping by and bringing food. Becky came over to visit them. She looked terrible. Her face was white, and her bandage seemed huge. She couldn't stop sobbing the whole time she was there, and finally, Pam took her home. Becky kept saying how sorry she was, and how she couldn't live without him, which only mirrored the others' pain.

The next day was worse somehow, because with each passing hour, it became more real. They went to the funeral home that night, and the next day the room they had chosen for him there was filled with friends, and relatives, and other kids. His graduation had been that day, and they had talked about him.

There had been a moment of silence for him, and everyone in the auditorium had cried for all of them.

The funeral was on Tuesday, and Alice had never been in so much pain in her life. Afterward, she couldn't even remember it. All she could remember were the flowers, the sound of singing in the distance somewhere, and looking at her shoes. She had clutched Bobby's hand the entire time, and Charlotte had cried uncontrollably. Jim had sat there crying and looking glazed. The high school principal spoke at the funeral for Johnny, as did his best friend. And the minister gave a beautiful eulogy about the remarkable boy he was, how bright, how kind, how wonderful, and how loved. But even the words were not enough to dim the pain. Nothing could soothe the agony they all felt. Nothing could change the fact that Johnny was dead.

And after they left him at the cemetery, it felt like the end of the world to them, when the Petersons got home.

There was nothing to comfort them in any of it, nothing to cling to, or to negotiate or bargain with. He had been taken from them in the blink of an eye. Too fast, too soon, too hard, too sad. Too overwhelming, and too agonizing to bear. And yet, whether they felt equal to it or not, it had to be borne. They had to live through it, and go on without him. There was no other choice.

Charlotte cried herself to sleep that night. And Bobby lay silent and alone in his room. He had cried all day too, but he was exhausted and fell asleep finally. And Alice and Jim sat downstairs, staring into space, thinking of their lost son, grappling with it, wrestling with the impossible concept that he was gone and would never return. It was truly unthinkable. Unbearable. Neither of them wanted to go up to bed, they were too afraid of their own thoughts and dreams. They just sat there all night. And finally at three o'clock, Alice went to bed. Jim stayed downstairs and drank all night, and in the morning she found him passed out on the couch, with an empty bottle of gin lying on the floor. It was the beginning of a ghastly time for all of them, and Alice couldn't imagine a time when life would seem normal to them again. Normal was Johnny coming home at night after work, going off to college in the fall, being valedictorian of his class, and playing on the football team; kissing him and hugging him, being able to look up at him and smile, or laugh with him, hold his hand, or touch his hair. There was nothing even remotely normal about his being gone. And as each day wore on, Alice grew more certain that their lives would never be normal again.

Chapter Three

Johnny had been gone for a month on the Fourth of July. Alice had had the photographs developed from the night of the prom. And when she did, the pictures of him smiling in his tux nearly broke her heart. She had had three of them framed and put them in Charlotte's and Bobby's rooms, and her own. Sometimes she thought seeing the photograph of him made things worse. He looked so handsome, and so young, and so alive.

The Fourth was a grim day for the Petersons that year. The barbecue they gave every year was a thing of the past. Seeing their friends would only have reminded them of the funeral, and it didn't seem appropriate to celebrate anything. There was nothing to celebrate or enjoy, nothing to smile about. Their house had been deadly quiet for the past month. They all looked exhausted and drained, and sick. And they were. Just surviving each day was like climbing Everest, and when they met at the dinner table every night, it was shocking to each of them to see how bad the others looked.

Alice had lost fourteen pounds and had dark circles under her eyes. And she admitted to Pam Adams, when she called every day, that she literally no longer slept at night. She fell asleep around six in the morning every day, and was awake again an hour later, by seven or eight. Sometimes she fell asleep in a chair. And Jim lay on the couch, drinking all night until he passed out. Charlotte cried constantly, as they all did. She didn't want to leave the house, and had missed the entire month's baseball games. Bobby hadn't been this withdrawn since he nearly drowned. They were all in extreme pain.

And Becky was no better, Pam said. She wouldn't get out of bed for the first week, and when she finally went back to work, she was so upset they sent her home. She had finally managed to work part time the week before, she seemed to cry constantly, seldom ate, and said that she wished she had died with him. The rest of the Adams children were sad for her, and worried about her, and they missed Johnny. He had been their friend too.

"You've got to get some sleep," Pam said to Alice practically. "You will eventually. The same thing happened to me when I lost Mike. But you don't want to get sick before you start sleeping again. What about sleeping pills?" She had taken them for a while, but she didn't like the hangover she had all day, so she had finally just toughed it out, which was what Alice said she wanted to do.

"Will I always feel like this?" Alice asked, feeling panicked again. It was hard to imagine spending the rest of one's life in that much pain.

"I think it's different with a child. And you never forget. But it changes eventually. You learn to live with it. Like a limp." She hadn't gotten over Mike yet, and it had been two years. But she managed to get up every day now, and laugh sometimes, and take care of her kids. She didn't tell Alice that there was no longer any real joy in her life. Her friends were still telling her that there would be again one day. "It won't be this bad forever. Alice, it's only been a month. How are the kids?"

"Charlie started playing baseball again yesterday, but she left halfway through. The coach has been really great about it. He says she can do whatever she wants, play, sit it out, just watch if she wants. He lost a sister at her age, and he says he knows what it's like."

"What about Bobby?"

"He seems completely shut down. He just lies on his bed all day. He won't even come downstairs to eat. I have to carry him. Jim thinks I shouldn't baby him, but," she broke down in sobs again as she tried to explain it to her friend, they were closer now than they'd ever been, and Alice had come to rely on talking to her every day, "in a way, Bobby and Charlotte are all I have left. Jim is never here, and when he is . . . well . . . you know how he is . . . he just anesthetizes himself so he doesn't have to feel anything. He doesn't even want to talk about him. He thinks I should clean out his room and give everything away. I just can't do that yet. Maybe I never will. I go in and sit in there sometimes. It's as though, if I sit there long enough, and wait for him, he'll come home. I haven't even changed his sheets. That must sound crazy to you," Alice said apologetically, but Pam knew it only too well.

"I kept Mike's clothes for over a year, and I still have some of his favorite things."

"I just wasn't prepared for this," Alice said miserably. "Maybe I never will be.

It never occurred to me that he could die, that something like this could happen to us. This happens to other people. I never thought it would happen to me . . . or to any of us. . . ." It was almost exactly the way Pam herself had felt when her husband died unexpectedly. But losing a boy like Johnny at seventeen was even more of a travesty. Becky had even said that herself. Johnny had left a lot of broken hearts behind, but it wasn't his fault. Some people had told Alice that she'd be angry at him one day, for leaving them, but she couldn't imagine it. His death had certainly not been his fault. And no matter how shattered they were by it, by no stretch of the imagination could she blame her son.

They had all been planning to go to the lake in late July, but they canceled their plans and stayed home. By August, Alice was still awake all night, but at least Jim was drinking less. He had gone back to drinking beer in front of the TV at night, and had stopped drinking gin.

Charlotte was playing baseball again, and Alice had asked Jim to go to her games, just to show her some support after everything that had happened to them, but he said he didn't have time. And Bobby was still lying on his bed most of the time. Despite all of Alice's efforts to lure him downstairs with her, and keep him entertained, the moment her back was turned, or she answered the phone, or did anything, he went back upstairs to his bed. The house was like a tomb at night, they each kept to themselves, nursing their wounds, and thinking of him. And for a while every afternoon, Alice sat in Johnny's room.

And when Pam took a good look at her in early September, she thought Alice looked worse than she had since June. Johnny had been gone for three months by then, but for his mother nothing had changed. She was as grief-stricken as she had been in the first few days after his death, and she could barely make herself get dressed every day. When she did, she wore jeans and a sweater with holes in it. She looked every bit as depressed as she felt. Pam even offered to do her hair for her, but Alice just shook her head and said she didn't care.

The kids had gone back to school again when she started getting stomach pains. They were fierce and sharp, and she finally mentioned it to Jim one night and he looked concerned.

"You'd better go to the doctor right away." They were all frightened about each other now. Their own mortality had been underlined. Alice worried about Charlotte now constantly, getting hurt while she played, or hit by a car on her way to school on her bike. The concept of invulnerability had been permanently dispelled.

"I think I'm okay," Alice said unconvincingly. She was more worried about the kids. Charlotte had gotten two migraines that week, and had to come home from school. And Bobby wouldn't go to school at all. He locked himself in his room so he wouldn't have to go, and the principal of his school had said to wait another month and see how things went.

The stomach pains got worse over the next few weeks, but she didn't say anything. She knew she had to be strong for the rest of them, and she said as much to Pam. Becky was still in bad shape too. She was working full time again, but all she did was sit at home and cry at night. She never saw her friends anymore, or went anywhere. Johnny had left them all in sorry shape.

The kids had been back in school for a month, when Alice lay in bed next to Jim one night, trying not to shout out in pain. She was in so much agony, she could hardly think, and just after he came to bed, she began vomiting, and as soon as she did, she saw bright spots of blood. Her old nursing experience told her just how bad it was. She stayed in the bathroom for a long time, vomiting and when she finally opened the door, she could hardly stand up. Jim was still awake, though a little less than alert, but he sobered up quickly when he saw her face. She was no longer even white. She was green.

"Alice? Are you okay?" He was sitting up in bed, and staring at her, with a look of panic on his face.

"No," she said softly, doubled over with pain. She couldn't even walk by then, and as she looked at him, the room whirled around, and she began sliding slowly to the floor.

"Alice! . . . Alice. . . ." He rushed to her, as she passed out, and then he ran to the phone and dialed 911. She looked as though she were dead, and he could feel his heart pound as they answered and he told them his wife was unconscious, and she had been vomiting. He realized suddenly as he looked at her how much weight she had lost. And it suddenly occurred to him that she might die too. He couldn't even conceive of losing her. And as he spoke to the emergency operator, Alice stirred and began vomiting

again. She never fully regained consciousness, but he saw bright pools of
blood.

"We'll get an ambulance out right
away." And, minutes later, as he knelt
next to her, he could hear the siren of
the ambulance, and ran to let the paramedics in. He took the stairs two at a
time as he led them upstairs, and as
they hurried into the room, Charlotte
came out into the hall, looking terrified. Mercifully, by then Bobby was
sound asleep.

"What's wrong?" Charlotte asked
with a look of panic on her face, as she
watched the paramedics bending over
her mom. Even Charlie could see that
Alice was gray, and she started to cry as
they worked over her mother's lifeless
form. "What happened, Dad?" she
asked, crying uncontrollably.

"I don't know," he said in a choked
voice. "She's been vomiting blood." He
didn't even think to reassure Charlotte,
he was too worried about his wife to
think of her. He had no time for anyone

but Alice now. He wanted to hear what the paramedics had to say.

"It could be a number of things," they explained, "most likely a bleeding ulcer. We've got to take her right in. Will you come with us?" they asked, as they put her on a stretcher and covered her. Even in her unconscious state, she was shivering, and slipping rapidly into shock from the blood she'd lost.

"I'll be right there," Jim said, pulling on his pants, and slipping into shoes without socks. He put on a sweater, grabbed the phone, and called Pam. He told her what was happening, and asked her if she could come and stay with the kids until he got home. He hated to impose on her, but he couldn't think of who else to call.

"Just go with her. I'll be over in five minutes. Don't worry about the kids. Becky can stay with mine here. Just take care of Alice, Jim. I've been worried about her for a long time." They had all seen how much weight she had lost, but no one said anything. They knew why, and how hard it was for her to come back to life again. It had been the worst four months of her life since Johnny died in June.

Jim climbed into the ambulance with her, without saying a word to his kids before he left. And Charlotte sat huddled in her parents' bed like a lost child. Pam found her there, and hugged her tight. And then she checked on Bobby, when she could leave Charlie finally, but he was still sound asleep, much to her relief. She made warm milk for Charlie after that, cleaned up the blood on the bedroom carpet, and they sat at the kitchen table, talking for hours. About how miserable life was without Johnny now, how upset her parents had been, how much her father drank, and how destroyed her mother was. Charlie told Pam that their lives would never be the same again, and Pam admitted that was true, but it would be a lot better again one day. It wouldn't always be like this, and in time Alice would make her peace with it, and be able to turn her full attention to them again. For the moment, she was being crippled by grief, but Pam assured Charlotte that it was a process and not an end.

Pam called the hospital after she got Charlotte to bed, and she talked to Jim. They were still working on Alice then. She was being given powerful medications by IV, they had sedated her, and they were giving her two units of blood. She wasn't out of the woods yet, by any means. She had regained consciousness once, briefly, but the last time he had seen her she was unconscious again. He said she was in a private room next to the ICU, and there was an ICU nurse with her. The doctors were checking on her constantly, and they wouldn't let him stay in the room. He could only go in for five minutes every half-hour. And when he did, Alice looked terrible to him.

"What exactly do they say is wrong with her?" Pam sounded desperately worried as she listened to him, and he sounded sober and scared beyond belief.

"She has an ulcer apparently. They think the bleeding has stopped now. But if I hadn't gotten her here as fast as we did, she could have died."

"I know," Pam said quietly. "Thank God you did."

"Thanks for staying with the kids, Pam," he said, sounding drained. "I'll call and let you know how things are here."

"Call me anytime. I'll grab the phone as soon as it rings, so it doesn't wake the kids."

"Thanks, Pam," he said again, and went back to his wife. The nurse told him she was sedated and would sleep for hours, and they offered him a bed in the waiting room, for the night. He didn't want to leave her there, and seemed grateful to stay. And as soon as he lay down on the cot they'd given him, he fell asleep. He was exhausted from the strain of worrying about her, and by then it was the middle of the night.

Alice was sleeping more peacefully by then, and she hadn't vomited again. Her blood pressure was slightly higher than it had been, and the nurse came in every twenty minutes now to check her vital signs, but they were satisfied that she wasn't about to die. They left her alone in the room for twenty minutes at a time, and she was in a deep sleep, filled with complicated dreams. She couldn't tell where the dreams were leading her, but after a while, she was aware that Johnny was walking along at her side. He seemed happy and at ease, and after a while, he turned toward her with a smile and said, "Hi, Mom." It was just the way he had looked every night when he came home from Becky's house after work, and she had dinner waiting for him.

"Hi, sweetheart, how've you been?" Alice was aware of being able to talk to him in the dream, and she noticed how well and happy he looked and she was glad. She felt more awake than asleep, but she knew she had to be asleep if she was seeing him. She also knew she didn't want the dream to end.

"I'm fine, Mom. But you're not in such great shape. What have you been doing to yourself?" She could see the worry in his big brown eyes. He was wearing a clean blue shirt, and jeans, and his favorite shoes, and she wondered how he had managed to take them with him. She distinctly remembered, even in her dream, burying him in a different pair, and his one dark suit. But the mystery of what he was wearing seemed too deep to solve.

"I'm okay," she reassured him, "I just miss you a lot." She had an odd sense that she wasn't actually saying anything, but talking to him in her head. And she wasn't sure how.

"I know you miss me, Mom," he said gently. "But that's no excuse to fall apart. Charlie's really sad these days, and Bobby is a mess."

"I know they are. I don't know what to do for them."

"Dad needs to start going to her games, even if she is a girl. She's a better athlete even than I was. And Bobby's not listening to you anymore. You have to do something about it, Mom, or he's going to slip into a worse place." He was already nearly autistic now, and she had been worrying about the same thing.

"Why don't you talk to Dad?" she said sensibly, and he smiled. She could see him perfectly with her eyes closed, and she could hear him in her head.

"He can't hear me, Mom. You can." She knew Johnny was right because this was her dream, not Jim's. "You've got to get well now, Mom. You can't do anything for anyone until you do that. You have to get well and go home." She could hear his voice with perfect clarity in the stillness in her head.

"I don't want to go home," she said miserably and started to cry in the dream. "I hate being home without you now. It makes me too sad." He stood watching her for a long time, not sure what to say to her, as she cried. He put an arm around her, and she blew her nose. "I'm never going to get used to this," she said, trying to explain it to him, as though it would make a difference now and he could change his mind, and come back, if she talked sensibly to him.

"Yes, you will," Johnny said emphatically, "you're very strong, Mom." He sounded very firm.

"No, I'm not," she sobbed. "I can't be strong for everyone, your father, myself, Charlie, and Bobby. I don't have anything left to give."

"Yes, you *do*," Johnny insisted, and then there was a sound in her dream, like another voice talking to her. This one seemed to come from far away, and she didn't recognize it. She opened her eyes to see who it was. It was the nurse. And as she looked at her, her sense of Johnny talking to her disappeared.

"You're having mighty busy dreams tonight, aren't you?" the nurse said pleasantly, taking her blood pressure again, and looking pleased by what she saw. Things were looking better for

Alice again. But for a while there it had been a close call.

Alice closed her eyes and went to sleep again, and as soon as she did, she found the dream. And it was comforting to find Johnny waiting for her as soon as she did. He was sitting on a low wall, swinging his feet, as he had done as a little kid. And he hopped off the wall as soon as he saw her again, but as soon as she spoke to him, he didn't like what he heard.

"Johnny, I want to come with you." She had been waiting to say that to him for four months. And now she could in the dream. It had been in the back of her mind for a while, but she had never actually formulated the words, or admitted it to herself. She wanted to be with him. She couldn't live without him anymore.

"Are you out of your mind?" Johnny looked shocked. "And leave Bobby, Charlie, and Dad? No way. They need you too much. I don't make the decisions around here, but I can tell you no one here would buy that idea. Forget it, Mom. Shape up." He sounded angry at her.

"I can't do it without you," Alice said unhappily. "I don't want to be here."

"I don't care. You still have work to do. And so do I," he said, sounding far more grown-up than he had when he left.

"What kind of work do you have to do?" his mother asked him, sounding curious, but he shrugged. He was sitting on the wall again, swinging his feet.

"I don't know. They haven't told me yet. Something tells me it's going to be a big job, given your attitude and the shape you're in. How can you be like this, Mom? You've never been a quitter before." He sounded disappointed in her, and she looked up into the familiar eyes and wished she could touch his face, but something told her she could not. She knew instinctively that if she did, she might wake up.

"You've never been dead before. I can't take this, sweetheart. I just can't."

He hopped off the wall and stood looking at her as she said the words. He
seemed angry and sounded very firm
when he spoke again.

"I don't ever want to hear you say
that again. Behave yourself." He
sounded more like the father than the
child, and seemed suddenly very
grown-up. And even Alice was aware
that it was a very odd dream. It had a
strange feeling of reality to it, as though
she were in a different world with him.

"All right, all right," she felt and
sounded like a kid as he scolded her and
she answered him. "You don't know
how hard it is, being here without
you." She had wanted to say that to him
for months, and was relieved that she
could now.

"I know. I hated leaving so fast. It
came as a surprise. And poor Becky. I
hated leaving her too." He looked sorrowful as he thought of it, and Alice's
heart ached for him.

"She's doing a little better now," his
mother reassured him, and he nodded,

as though he knew more about it than she did.

"She's going to be fine. She just doesn't know it yet. And so will you, and Charlie, and Bobby, and Dad. If you'd just do what you have to do to get over it, and if Dad would go to Charlie's games, things might get better a little faster than they are. You guys sure aren't making this any easier for me," he said, looking a little tired, and very concerned. She noticed that he seemed to be fading a little as she talked to him, as though he'd stayed long enough and was worn out.

"I'm sorry, sweetheart. I didn't mean to let you down," she said apologetically, hoping the dream wasn't about to end. She had an odd sense that he was going to slip away and she was about to wake up.

"You never have let me down, Mom. And I know you won't now. Right now, just get well, and then we'll talk about the other stuff."

"When?" She wanted to know when

she'd see him again. She had never had a dream like this since he died.

"I told you, when you get well. Right now, I don't want you to worry about anything."

"Why not?"

"Because you're sick, and I don't have my assignment yet anyway." He was speaking cryptically, and she was confused. But they were still strolling along, and he looked as real as he ever had.

"What assignment?"

"Don't worry about it, Mom." He looked very adult as he spoke to her, and she was relieved to see how well he was.

"Are you in school?"

"I guess you could call it that. Maybe I have to earn my wings." As soon as he had said it, he laughed. And then he gave her a kiss and walked off, and she wanted to run after him, but suddenly she found she couldn't follow him. It was as though a wall had come up, and she had to stop. She watched him disappear, but she didn't feel as sad as she had, and when the nurse woke her up the next time she took Alice's blood pressure, she smiled when she woke up. It had been the most beautiful dream she'd ever had.

"You look like you're feeling better, Mrs. Peterson," the nurse said, looking pleased, and after she left, Alice drifted off to sleep again, but this time she didn't see Johnny in her dreams. And that morning when Jim came to see her with the kids before he left to get dressed for work and they went to school, she almost told them about the dream she'd had, and then thought better of it. She didn't want to frighten them, and she sensed that she should keep it to herself. It was hard talking about things like that with Jim anyway, and she suspected that Bobby was afraid of ghosts.

The doctor decided to have her stay in the hospital one more night, and Pam came to see her that afternoon, and they talked for a while. And Jim called to tell her that he had decided to stay home that night with the kids. Alice reassured

him that she was fine, and that night
when she went to sleep, she saw Johnny
in her dreams again. She loved the new
dimension she'd discovered with him,
and she wanted to sleep all the time.
And he seemed happy and in a great
mood, and they talked about a lot of
things, Becky, and school, the jobs he
had had over the years, and why his father drank so much. They both knew it
was because of the accident five years
before, but Johnny said it had been long
enough, and it was time he stopped. It
was as though Johnny had suddenly become wise beyond his years.

"That's easier said than done," Alice
said to her son quietly. "I don't like it either, but as long as Bobby can't talk,
your father is going to be consumed
with guilt."

"He'll talk one of these days, when
he's ready to. And then Dad won't have
any excuse anymore."

"What makes you think Bobby will
talk?" She had given up all hope of that
about two years before. They had done

everything they could for him, and nothing had improved or changed. Nor would it now, she felt sure.

"He just will. You'll see."

"Do you have that from a higher source, or are you just trying to cheer me up?" she asked, smiling at him. It felt so good to see Johnny again, even if only in a dream.

"Both. Actually, I just know it in my heart. I can always hear him in my head. I always did."

"I know," she said sadly, thinking of her younger son, and the trauma he had had, "and no one else does."

"I think you could hear him too, if you tried," Johnny said, and she considered it for a while. It was an intriguing thought. She had never tried. She just filled in the blanks for him, but it had never occurred to her to listen to Bobby in her head, as Johnny had done.

"I'll try it when I go home," she promised, wondering if that was why she had seen Johnny in the dream, if that had been his message for her. Or maybe it was what they had given her in the hospital. Maybe the medications were making her imagine things. And she had a sense, as they were talking, that it was nearly morning by then. She dreaded waking up and losing him again. She hated mornings now. She would wake up with a lead ball on her chest, remembering that something terrible had happened to them, and within seconds, as she opened her eyes, she knew just what it was. Johnny was gone.

"I don't want to lose you again," she said sadly, as his pace slowed down again. "Can't I just stay here with you?" All she wanted was to be with him.

"Of course not, Mom, you're not dead. And you're not going to be for a long time. You've still got too much work to do here." He sounded firm.

"I miss you so much." She could barely say the words, they hurt so much.

"I miss you too, Mom," he said quietly. "A lot. I miss Becky too . . . and

Bobby . . . and Charlie . . . and Dad. It's hard to get used to not being with you. But I'm going to be around for a while."

"You are?" She was surprised, and he smiled.

"I have an assignment to do," he said mysteriously.

"You do?" She looked confused. "Like what?"

"I don't know. They don't tell you that part. You have to figure it out. They don't give you details. I think it just kind of . . . unfolds."

"What do you mean?" She was puzzled by what he'd said.

"I'm not sure myself, Mom. I think I just do what I feel like I'm supposed to do . . . and when everything gets done, I can go." It seemed pretty simple, as long as he could figure out what he was supposed to do in the correct amount of time.

"I don't understand. And what happens now when I wake up? Will I have this dream again when I go back to sleep?" It made her want to sleep forever, just so she could see him.

He laughed at the question she asked, and it was the laugh she remembered so well, and the smile she had missed so much. It felt so good to see him again, and made her feel more than ever that she didn't want to wake up.

"I think you'll be seeing me a lot." He didn't mention the dream.

"When?" She wanted answers from him, and promises that she'd see him again in her dreams. The past two nights had been like a gift from him. It was exactly like being with him.

"Now," he said comfortably. He seemed completely at ease with her.

"What do you mean *now*?"

"I mean now, when you wake up."

"I'll see you when I wake up?" Even she knew better than that.

He nodded again, and she stared at him, confused.

"How about explaining that?"

"Okay. Wake up."

"Now?"

"Yeah, now. Open your eyes."

"I don't want to open my eyes. If I wake up now, you'll be gone, and everything will be awful again. I refuse to wake up." She sounded more like a child than her son, and wanted to squeeze her eyes shut as tightly as she could.

"Wake up, Mom. Open your eyes." She tried to resist at first, and then found that she could not. It was as though he were compelling her to do as he said. Her eyes fluttered open, and she couldn't see clearly at first in the darkened room, but when her eyes adjusted, she could see Johnny sitting at the end of her bed, looking just exactly as he had in her dream.

"Wow, this is some terrific dream," she said, looking at him with a grin. "It must be the drugs." She was amused. Maybe it was a hallucination, not a dream.

"No, it's not the drugs, Mom," he said confidently, getting the hang of it himself. "It's me."

"What do you mean, it's you?" She was suddenly staring right at him, and her eyes were open. It didn't make any sense to her. It no longer felt like a dream. And she was totally confused. She could see Johnny talking to her, and she had the impression she was wide awake, which was completely weird.

"Just what I said, Mom, it's me. This is pretty cool, Mom, isn't it?" He looked thrilled, and there was a look of panic in her eyes. She was suddenly wondering if she was delusional. Maybe her grief for him had finally pushed her over the edge. "I'm coming back for a while, Mom. But only to you," he said, trying to explain it to her while her eyes grew wider still. "I think this is kind of a special deal. Someone told me it happens to people who leave very suddenly, and need to tie up loose ends. All I know is that you're supposed to fix things for people. But no one told me what to fix, or exactly for who. I think you have to figure it out for yourself."

"John Peterson," his mother said,

trying to look stern, as she sat in her hospital bed and stared at him, "have you been doing drugs up there?" She looked utterly confused. She had inadvertently become part of a phenomenon that defied everything she believed or knew. It was like an out-of-body experience that included Johnny, and he looked happy, and at ease, and real. "I don't understand what's going on," she said, looking a little wan. "I still think it must be the drugs I'm taking," she said to herself, as a nurse walked into the room, and Johnny disappeared. It was as though he had never been there at all, but this time, she didn't feel sad. He had seemed far too real, and for once, she didn't feel the weight of a crushing loss. She felt oddly cheered.

"And how are you today?" the nurse asked happily, and was pleased once again with Alice's vital signs. She only stayed for a few minutes, and then left the room again. Alice closed her eyes, thinking of her son, and when she opened them, Johnny was standing next to her bed, grinning at her.

"This can't be happening," she said, smiling up at him. "But I'm loving every minute of it. Where did you go?"

"I can't hang around when there are other people in the room. Those are the rules. I told you, Mom, I'm only here for you."

"I wish you were," she said with a yawn, but never taking her eyes off him. This was getting harder and harder to understand, and better and better to feel. It was so great seeing him, or thinking that she did.

"I am here for you, Mom. Trust me. I told you, this is very cool."

"What are you saying to me?" She felt suddenly nervous now, as though something important were happening to her, far, far beyond her control, or even his. And it was.

"I know this will sound weird to you. It did to me too at first. They're sending me back for a while, to do some special work. Because when I went, I left so fast, I didn't have time to finish things. So they're letting me do it now. Not for me, but for everyone else. I think . . . you . . . Bobby . . . Charlie . . . Dad . . . Becky too, probably . . . maybe her mom . . . I've got a lot of stuff to do, but they haven't explained it to me yet."

"Are you telling me you're coming back?" She sat bolt upright in bed and stared at him. And this time she knew she wasn't asleep.

"Just for a while," he said, looking pleased.

"Are you telling me I'm really seeing you, and this isn't some crazy drug they gave me in my IV that's making me hallucinate?"

"No, it's bigger than that, Mom. A lot bigger." He grinned again. "It's pretty good stuff. I know I'm going to like it. I've missed you all so much."

"So have I," she said as tears filled her eyes, and instinctively she reached out for his hand, and he took hers in his own. It felt just as it always had, and he looked no different than before. He was still the same beautiful boy he had always been, her beloved older son. "You mean I get to see you all the time again?" she asked with a look of disbelief and a lump in her throat.

"Pretty much. Except when I'm busy doing something else. I told you, I'm going to have a lot to do. It sounds like a big job."

"Can anyone else see you?"

"No, just you. I was kind of hoping Becky could see me too, but they don't think that's a good idea. This is kind of like a big favor to you, Mom. I think you should say thank you or something, when you get the chance." She just nodded, looking at him, unable to believe what he had just said.

"I will," she whispered to him. "I will. . . ." And then suddenly she had doubts again. "Are you sure I didn't just go nuts in here . . . or they're giving me psychedelics that'll wear off when I get home?"

"I'm sure, Mom. Why don't you rest

for a while? I've got some things to do. I'll see you when you get home." He leaned over and kissed her then, and she felt his warmth next to her. And as soon as he had kissed her, he smiled at her, and then as though she had blinked and lost him again, he was gone. But it didn't feel the same this time. She knew she hadn't lost him, and she still wasn't sure what had happened, but whatever it was, her heart was lighter than it had been in four months, or ever before.

She lay in bed, thinking about him, feeling the warmth he had left with her, and she remembered what he had just said, and as she closed her eyes, seeing her son in her mind's eye, and remembering his kiss, his touch, she silently whispered, "Thanks."

They brought her breakfast in after that, and she ate decently for once. A lot more than she had in months. Oatmeal and toast and coffee and a soft-boiled egg, and all she wanted to do was smile and laugh every time she thought about him. She wasn't sad anymore, or devastated, or crushed, or depressed. She was happier than she'd been in years. The doctor thought her recovery miraculous. He still wanted her to take the medication he'd given her, until her ulcer healed, but after he had checked her over carefully, he said she could go home. And she smiled as soon as he said the words, because she knew who would be waiting for her there. And if it was all a dream, and that was all it turned out to be, she knew with absolute certainty that it was the best one she had ever had.

Chapter Four

Jim came to pick Alice up from the hospital that afternoon on his lunch hour, and took her home. She was in good spirits, and a little stronger than she'd been. And she had promised her doctor she would rest. One of her neighbors came to visit her after she got home, and Pam came by with Becky that night, to see how she was. She was on a special diet, and Charlotte had cooked dinner for all of them.

Alice put on her bathrobe and went downstairs. Jim even ate dinner with them that night, and sat with them for a little while, before disappearing into the living room to watch TV with a six-pack of beer. Alice helped Charlotte do the dishes and clean up, and Bobby sat silently at the kitchen table, watching them. He hadn't taken his eyes off his mother since she got home. He had been terrified when he realized that she was gone, and sure that she would never come back again. And when she went back upstairs to her room, he followed her, and sat down on the end of her bed.

"It's okay, sweetheart, I'm not going anywhere. I'm fine. Honest." She could see in Bobby's big blue eyes that he was still scared. The memory of Johnny leaving them so suddenly was still fresh for all of them, Bobby particularly, and after a while, he came to sit next to her on the bed and held her hand.

It was only after she had put him to bed that she heard a sound in her room, and thought that Charlotte had wandered in to borrow something to wear, as she often did. She was taller than Alice, and narrower, but she still managed to borrow her fair share of sweaters and accessories to wear with her favorite pair of jeans.

"Charlie?" Alice said in the direction of her closet, as she got back into bed, and then jumped when she saw Johnny smiling at her. He was wearing the same blue shirt and clean pair of jeans he'd been wearing when she saw him in the hospital, and his hair was as neat and freshly trimmed as it had been the night of the prom.

"Hi, Mom," he said, and bent over her to kiss her on the cheek, and then sat down on the end of her bed, as he often had when he wanted to talk to her.

"It's going to take me a while to get used to this," she admitted to him. "It's something of a miracle, isn't it?"

"Yes, it is." He nodded, still smiling at her.

"What did you do today?" she asked, casually, sinking back against her pillows, and savoring the sight of him. He looked so good, so young and strong, so confident, even more than he had before. He used to get a little worried frown sometimes, and now he just looked happy all the time. And then she realized how odd it sounded to ask him what he'd done. It was as though he had never left, and she expected him to tell her about work, or school.

"I went to see Becky today. She looked so sad." His eyes grew more serious as he said the words. He had followed her for hours, and watched her with the kids and talking to her mom.

"She and her mom came by for a while."

"I know, Mom. I was here."

"You were?"

He nodded then, and seemed to be thinking about something else. "Bobby is really scared about you," he explained to her, but she already knew. Bobby didn't need words to tell her how he felt, and the way he had stayed with her all day had told her everything she needed to know. Bobby was terrified she'd die too.

"I think he was afraid I wouldn't come back from the hospital. Like you," she said diplomatically.

"I know, Mom," Johnny said quietly.

"And Charlie is upset about Dad." Alice nodded, there was nothing she could say to that. She was worried about him too. His drinking had gotten markedly worse ever since Johnny had died. All she could do was hope that he'd lighten up on his drinking again. But in recent weeks it had only gotten worse. He never got so drunk he couldn't go to work the next day. And he never drank until he got home. But once he began, he drank steadily all night, and by the time he came to bed, he was blind and numb. It was no way to live. And it affected all of them, as she knew. But he wouldn't let her talk to him, and she couldn't see anymore how it could change. She never told anyone, and she had gotten good at explaining it away, and making excuses for him, particularly to the kids. But it was no secret to anyone in the house what was happening to him, or why. First, he had nearly drowned his younger son, in an accident that left him mute, and then he had lost his favorite son. It was more than he could tolerate, or bear to think about. And when he drank, he didn't have to feel, or think anything at all. It was the perfect escape for him.

"What's going to happen now?" Alice looked at her son curiously. She had been wondering about it all day, still unsure if what she had seen of him was real or a dream. It was pretty remarkable, and would have been impossible to explain to anyone. And she would never have tried. "How does this work? Are you going to be around all the time, or just kind of come and go?" The oddest thing was that they were speaking normally and she wondered if anyone would hear them if they wandered by. They were going to have to be careful about that, or people were going to think she was crazy, talking to herself, since they couldn't see him.

"I guess I just kind of come in and out, while I do my work. I want to spend some time with Becky too." There was something sad in his eyes this time as he spoke to her. It had touched him when he saw how subdued Becky was that day. It brought home to him how many people had been affected when he left, but it was why he had come home again. There were too many loose ends, too much left undone. And he knew he had a lot to do now in a short time.

He got up off her bed then, and walked to the door of her room, and then stood there smiling at her.

"It feels good to be home, Mom." Even if it was only for a little while. It felt good to both of them.

"It's wonderful to have you home, sweetheart. I've missed you so much." Her words didn't begin to express all she felt.

"Yeah," he said softly, "me too. I'm going to go downstairs now to see Dad."

"Can he see you too?" She looked surprised by what he said. She didn't think Jim could see him too. And Johnny laughed at her.

"Of course not, Mom. Are you kidding? He'd freak out."

"Yes, I think he would," she laughed with him.

"I just want to make sure he's okay. And there's some stuff I want to look for in my room. What happened to my varsity jacket? You didn't give it away, did you?"

"Of course not. I let Bobby try it on. I was saving it for him. I told him he could have it one day, and his eyes lit up. He's got a lot of growing to do until then." They exchanged a smile.

"Charlie might like to wear it in the meantime," he said generously. He had worn it constantly, he'd been so proud of it.

"I don't think Dad thinks anyone should wear it but you. It's in your closet. Everything is still there." She hadn't moved or changed or given away anything. With all his trophies and pennants and photographs and awards, the room was a shrine to him. She seldom went in anymore, although she had in the first few weeks, she just liked knowing it was there, like a part of him.

"Get some sleep. I'll see you in the morning, Mom." It was just the way it had been only a few months before, when he used to come and say good night to her, leave to call Becky, and then go to his room.

"Good night, sweetheart." She sat there quietly, thinking of him, and a few minutes later Charlotte strolled in. Her hair was wet, she had just put gel in it, and she looked at her mother with a quizzical air.

"Who were you talking to a minute ago? Was Dad up here?" They both knew Bobby was sound asleep. She had heard her mom saying something as she walked down the hall to her room, and she couldn't imagine who she was talking to.

"I was on the phone," Alice said without batting an eye. "Dad's still downstairs. He probably fell asleep."

"What else is new?" Charlie said with a disapproving air. "Peggy Dougal's dad used to be the same way . . . and he went to AA."

"Peggy Dougal's dad wound up in jail for drunk driving," Alice said defensively, "and he lost his job. He had to go to AA, the court sent him there. That's not the same thing." She had suggested it to Jim several times since the accident years before, and he always brushed her off or barked at her. He saw no need to go to AA, and always said he just liked to enjoy a few beers. And Alice knew she couldn't push him into it unless he was ready to go. It was up to him. And nothing she could say to him would make him see what everyone else did.

"Maybe not the same as Peggy's dad, but have you ever tried talking to Dad at night, Mom? He can't even understand what you say." And more often than not, he slurred his words.

"I know, baby." Alice didn't know what to say to her. It was the first time Charlotte had implied that her father was a drunk. And Alice didn't have the heart to tell her she was wrong. She had always been honest with her, even now. And whether or not he needed AA, he

needed to forgive himself for the accident first, and accept the fact that he had
lost his son. But that didn't seem to be
happening. He seemed to be drifting
further and further away from all of
them. The only child he had ever re-
lated to was gone, and the other two
didn't seem to exist for him. Sometimes
Alice wondered if he even knew they
were there. He never talked to them, or
acknowledged them. And yet, he had
loved talking to Johnny for hours, about
sports and games and scores. He had no
one to talk to now, not even her. "It's
late, sweetheart, you should get to bed.
I'll go wake Dad in a while and bring
him upstairs."

"Doesn't it make you mad, Mom?"
she asked with a sorrowful air, as her
mother shook her head.

"No. Just sad sometimes." Charlotte
nodded, and walked slowly out of the
room, and then stopped just as Johnny
had, with her hand on the door.

"Are you okay, Mom? Are you feeling better now?"

"Much." The transfusions had worked wonders for her, and the medication had quieted the pain. But better than that, she was smiling again. In the oddest of ways, and for no reason she could understand, Johnny had come home, and she had hope again.

Chapter Five

*A*lice kept busy around the house for the next few days. She had plenty to do, and she had promised her doctor she would rest, which she did. Jim was dropping the kids off at school for her, and one of the other mothers was driving Bobby home. Charlotte knew her mom wasn't going to her basketball games that week, and said she understood. And Alice had all the time in the world to be at home, and talk to Johnny when he was there.

As he had said he would, he came and went, he wanted to see his friends, check out his old school. He had sat in on some of Charlotte's classes with her. He told their mother she was doing well, but was more interested in sports than her work, and he told his mother she really needed help in math. Other than that, he thought she seemed to be doing okay.

But Bobby was the one who worried him. He had visited him too, and he said he kept to himself, didn't seem to bond with anyone, and never joined in any of the games. Even in his special school, he was unusually withdrawn. He had been worse than ever, ever since Johnny died, and he had only gone back to school finally, just before Alice got sick.

"What are you going to do with him, Mom? I thought he'd be talking again by now." It didn't look like there was much chance of it, particularly after five years. And it was obvious that Johnny's death had driven the boy even further into himself.

"He still could talk one day," Alice said hopefully. "Maybe he'll want to say something to us enough to try." For the moment, he seemed to be comfortable as he was.

"What does the doctor say?"

She sighed, thinking about it. It was like the old days again, when she could talk to him. God knew, she couldn't talk to Jim. And Charlotte was still too young. "The doctor said he doesn't respond to the therapists, and there's no point pushing him. The last time we tried, he only got more withdrawn. He just can't do it, I guess." And sometimes she wondered what would happen to him when she was gone. He could learn to live a life on his own one day, she supposed, but his world was so limited, and always would be, if he didn't break through his walls. And for the time being, none of them had found the door, or the key.

"You ought to take him to Charlie's games. He used to love coming to mine," Johnny said sensibly, as Alice pondered it and then nodded. It was actually a good idea.

"He used to embarrass her, but she's grown up a lot since then. She probably wouldn't mind as much now."

"She'd better not," Johnny growled at her, and he kept her company in the kitchen while she baked two apple pies.

"Why two?" he asked, breathing deeply of the delicious fumes, as his mother shooed him away from the oven door. He wanted to open it so he could smell more.

"I thought I'd take one over to the Adamses this afternoon. They've been so good to us. Pam dropped off a couple of dinners for Dad while I was in the hospital. And they've been terrific to us ever since you died." The insanity of saying it to him suddenly made her stop and stare at him, and then they both laughed. "Do you realize how crazy this is? If anyone heard me talking to you like this, they'd probably lock me up."

"Well, no one's here to hear you, and they can't see me, so I guess everything's okay," he said, as she took a long drink of the supplement the doctor had prescribed for her. But ever since he had come back, she seemed to be feeling pretty good. Better than she had in years, in fact, and mostly thanks to him. It was amazing what the lightening of the yoke of grief did for her. She felt as though she had dropped twenty years, and looked it. She was only sorry the others couldn't see and talk to him too.

"I'd take the pies over to the Adamses for you if I could, Mom," he said casually, leaning against the refrigerator and watching her with a grin. "I don't think I can do stuff like that."

"This is miraculous enough, sweetheart," she said, still looking more than a little awed by what had happened to them. "Why do you think they sent you back?"

"I'm not sure. I think to finish things up. Supposedly, they do that sometimes when you go too fast, and leave a lot of unfinished stuff."

"Like what?"

"You . . . Dad . . . Bobby . . . Charlie . . . Becky . . . Maybe they thought none of you was doing so great, and needed some help."

"I guess we did," his mother said qui-

etly, grateful for these extra days with
him. They were an extraordinary gift,
and she was loving every minute of it.
"How long do you think they'll let you
stay?"

"As long as it takes," he said cryptically.

"To do what?" She still didn't understand what his "work" was going to be,
but neither did he.

"I don't know. Maybe I'm supposed
to figure it out for myself. They didn't
tell me much." She didn't dare ask him
who "they" were. He had no halo, no
wings, didn't fly, didn't come through
walls and doors. He was just walking
around as he always had, looking just
the way he did four months before,
hanging around in her kitchen, and sitting on the end of her bed. He looked
and felt and smelled and sounded the
same, and whenever she touched his
hand, or kissed his cheek, or put her
arms around him, he was warm. He was
the greatest gift she'd ever had, since
he'd returned, and she was unspeakably

grateful to have him there with her, for however long it was.

He was sitting in the living room, watching TV, when she left to pick Bobby up, and she asked him if he wanted to ride with her. He hesitated for a minute, and then decided that he would. And as they drove along, they talked about a number of things, the friends he'd had in school, the scholarship that had meant so much to him, the favorite games he'd played, the memories he had as a child that were so precious to all of them now. He made her laugh several times as they drove along, reminding her of pranks he'd played, and things she'd done. And she was still smiling when Bobby got into the car. And as soon as he did, Johnny disappeared.

"Hi, sweetheart. Did you have a good day?" Bobby nodded sometimes, but he didn't this afternoon. He just looked at her, and then glanced into the backseat, as though he sensed something there. And then he said nothing at all, and

looked out the window as they drove
away.

She gave him cookies and milk when
they got home, and he quietly went upstairs, when the phone rang and she answered it. It was Pam. She was still at
work, but wanted to share some gossip
with her. Alice said she'd baked an apple
pie for her, and Pam sounded pleased.
Alice promised to drop by with it after
Pam got home from work.

And when she did, she took Bobby
with her. The Adams kids were going
wild all over the kitchen and the living
room, and Becky was cooking dinner
for them with her long blond hair piled
high on her head. She looked a little
flustered as the hamburgers started to
burn, but Alice thought she was getting
more beautiful every day. It made it
doubly sad that Johnny was gone. They
would have been so happy when they
got married one day. And Becky hadn't
looked at anyone else in the four
months he'd been gone. At eighteen,
her life seemed as isolated as her mom's.

Becky felt widowed too, in her own way, and all she did was go to work, and come home to help take care of the kids. She hadn't even gone to a movie since Johnny had died. And Alice told her she should make an effort to get out sometime.

"I can't even get her to leave the house, except to go to work," Pam complained. She was worried about her. But she had been doing the same thing herself for the last two years since Mike had died.

"You both need to go out more. Why don't you let Charlie and me baby-sit for you sometime?" Alice wasn't entirely sure Charlotte would be pleased with the idea, but it would be nice to do something for them for a change.

The two women chatted for a while, and Bobby sat quietly watching the other kids. He didn't join in, and they didn't ask him to, although several of them were close to his age. But it was as though he weren't there. He was completely removed and withdrawn, and he seemed almost invisible to them as he watched everything they did. And as Alice turned at the sound of a particularly large crash from the living room, she saw Johnny following Becky up the stairs. Alice stared at him, startled to see him there, and when Becky came back to check on dinner again a few minutes later, he stood next to her at the stove. She was entirely unaware of him, as Alice struggled to listen to what Pam had just said. It was something about a man she'd met at work. But for the life of her, Alice couldn't remember what she'd said to her. Her eyes were riveted on Johnny, watching Becky butter the corn on the cob she'd made, and he turned to face his mother with a wave and a grin, as she smiled at him.

And when the Adams clan sat down to dinner a few minutes later, she and Bobby left. He went upstairs as soon as they got home, and Johnny was waiting for her at the kitchen table, smiling at her. She waited until she heard Bobby's door close, and then scolded him.

"What were you doing over there?"

"The same thing you were, Mom. Just visiting. God, Becky looks great."

"It was so weird watching you next to her. I couldn't even hear what Pam was saying to me." She still looked flustered as she thought about it, and Johnny laughed at her.

"I know. You should have seen the look on your face."

"They must have thought I was nuts. But not as nuts as if someone hears me talking to you. We have to be careful," she said, warning him, but he looked unconcerned.

"Sure, Mom, I know," he said, sounding like the seventeen-year-old he was. And a minute later, he bounded up the stairs and went off in the direction of Bobby's room. Alice was enjoying it, but it was certainly odd having him back in the house. And when Charlotte walked in after basketball practice, she gave her mother a strange look.

"How was your day?" Alice asked her, as she always did. The aura of normalcy she was trying to maintain was beginning to feel like a wig that had slipped.

"Okay," Charlotte answered, scrutinizing her, and then she finally decided to tell her mother what she'd heard. "Julie Hernandez's mom said she saw you in the car, talking to yourself, and laughing today. Mom, are you okay?" Charlie was beginning to wonder if the medication for her stomach was making her mom weird. She had heard her talk to herself the other night too, and her mom had said she'd been on the phone, but for some reason Charlotte didn't believe her.

"I'm fine. I was talking to Bobby. He was lying on the backseat," Alice explained.

"She said you looked like you were on your way *to* school."

"I think she was confused," Alice said comfortably as Charlotte shrugged her shoulders, only partially convinced. Her mom was definitely not herself these days. She was happier than she'd been in months, and looked almost guilty at times, as though she had done something she shouldn't have. And for a terrified instant, Charlotte couldn't help wondering if her mom had started drinking too. "How was your game?" Alice asked, as though nothing had been said.

"Okay, I guess. We won."

"You don't sound too excited about it," Alice said, focusing on her. Charlotte asked for so little from her, and she had been obscured at times by her brothers, the one such a hero, so much a star, and the other with his special needs. It was easy to lose track of Charlotte in the midst of it, and Alice was acutely aware of how unfair that was. She did her best to compensate for it, but lately Charlotte seemed to be avoiding everyone, and she was unusually withdrawn, even from her.

"I'm not excited about it," Charlotte said with a shrug, and then disappeared to use the phone.

Alice got dinner going then, and

eventually Jim came home. They went through the usual rituals, and as always now, dinner was a joyless meal, and went too fast. All any of them wanted to do was eat and run, and go to their own rooms. Jim parked himself in front of the TV afterward, and after she'd put the dishes away, Alice stopped for a minute to talk to him before she went upstairs to lie down on their bed. It had been a long day for her.

"Is everything all right at work?" she asked, as she sat down next to him on the couch.

"Fine," he said, without turning his eyes or his attention to her. "How do you feel?"

"Great." It was hard to believe that only a few days before she'd been so sick.

"Don't forget to take your medicine," he said, glancing at her, and she was touched by his concern. It was so rare that they talked now. They had been best friends once, and very much in love when they first married, but then things had never quite panned out for him, his business had never really gotten off the ground, and he had started drinking, not too much at first, but just enough to make a difference. And then he'd had the accident, and everything had changed after that. He had shut himself away in a place where Alice couldn't reach him anymore. But as he looked at her tonight, for just a fraction of a second, she saw the shadow of the man she still remembered and had always loved. "I'm glad you're feeling better. You really scared me. I couldn't . . ." He started to say something and then stopped himself. "We've had enough bad luck around here," he said gruffly, and then turned away to concentrate on the TV again, and before she could even answer him, he had dismissed her and disappeared.

"Thanks, Jim," she said, leaning over to kiss his cheek, but he pretended not to notice and didn't respond. He got up to get himself another beer, and left her sitting there. And he lingered in the kitchen just long enough for her to finally give up, and go upstairs, thinking about him.

She checked on both children, and they seemed fine. Bobby was throwing a ball against the wall in his room, and Charlotte was doing her homework. And as Alice walked back to her own room, she heard a sound in Johnny's room. She opened the door quietly, and saw him standing there in the moonlight, smiling at her. He had put on his beloved varsity jacket, as she walked in and closed the door softly behind her.

"What are you doing in here?" she whispered. Neither of them dared to turn the light on, for fear that someone would see.

"I'm just going through some stuff. I found some great pictures of Becky from last summer when she went to the lake with us."

"I see you found your jacket." He had grown so much in the last four years he had nearly outgrown it, but he loved it so much he didn't care even if the sleeves were a little short, and the shoulders tighter than they had been. "Why don't you go through that stuff tomorrow? Someone is going to hear you in here."

"I'll bet no one ever comes in here."

"I do," she said sadly, looking around the room and then at him. It was so good to see him back in it.

"How come you didn't put any of it away? I was afraid it would all be gone, or packed up in boxes somewhere."

"I couldn't do that," she said as her eyes held his.

"Maybe you should," he said sensibly. "It's kind of sad seeing it all sitting here like this . . . even though I'm glad you left it for me." She smiled at what he said, sat down on the bed, and looked up at him.

"I never thought you'd be back here. But how could I take apart this room? It would be like losing more of you than we already had."

"The room isn't me, Mom. You have me here," he said, pointing at his heart,

"and you always will. You know that."
He sat down next to her on the bed and
put an arm around her. "I'm not going
anywhere, even after I go back again. I'll
always be here with you."

"I know. But I love all this stuff . . .
your pictures . . . your trophies." The
room still smelled of him, even more so
now that he was sitting beside her. He
had a fresh clean smell, of soap and boy
and aftershave, that always made her
think of him, and lingered in the room.

They sat there talking for a while, and
eventually he went back to her bedroom with her, and the room was so
warm he took his jacket off and
dropped it on a chair, as they went on
talking. Charlotte came in once, and
looked at her oddly. She'd heard her
mother talking again, and was beginning to wonder about her. She wanted
to borrow a sweater to wear to assembly
the next day, and Johnny scolded his
mother when she left them and went
back to her room.

"You shouldn't let her wear your

stuff, Mom. All she wants to do is show off for the boys in her class, and the upperclassmen. Let her wear her own stuff."

"She's only got one mother. And I only have one daughter, Johnny. It's okay for her to borrow my 'stuff,' as long as she returns it."

"And does she?" He raised a cynical eyebrow at his mother, and she laughed, and looked at him sheepishly.

"Not always."

"Be careful if she borrows my varsity jacket. I don't want her to lose it." They had already agreed that it would go to Bobby eventually.

And after a while, he went back to his own room, to look around again, and she was putting on her nightgown when Jim came upstairs, and he looked startled, and frowned, when he saw Johnny's varsity jacket on the chair where he had left it.

"What's that doing here?"

"I . . . I was just looking at it," she said, turning away from him, so he wouldn't see her expression. Jim always knew when she was lying to him, which she rarely did.

"You shouldn't go in his room," he said firmly. "It'll just upset you."

"Sometimes it feels right to just sit there, with his things, and remember him," she said quietly, and he shook his head as he walked into the bathroom to put on his pajamas. He was a fairly modest man, but she had always liked that about him. In the days before he drank too much there had been a lot she had liked about him. And for some reason, in the last two days, those memories had come to mind more and more often. It was as though she was not seeing who he was, but remembering who he had been.

And when he came out of the bathroom, Jim reminded her to put the jacket away the next day, and leave it in Johnny's closet. "Don't let the kids play with it," he admonished her, "they'll just lose it. And it meant a lot to him."

"I know that. I promised him I'd save

it for Bobby," she said, not thinking how it sounded.

"When did you promise him that?" He looked puzzled.

"A long time ago. When he first got it."

"Oh," Jim nodded, satisfied with her explanation. He hated even seeing it there. It just reminded them of everything they had lost and would never have again. If he could have, he would have put it back in Johnny's room then, but he didn't want to go in there.

Jim got into bed next to her, and turned off the light, and the house was silent around them. Alice couldn't help wondering where Johnny was, if he had disappeared again to wherever he went these days between the times he spent chatting with her, or if he was still in his room, going through his papers, and rummaging in his desk. And she smiled, as she lay next to Jim, thinking of their son, and she was surprised when Jim put an arm around her. It was so rare that he was amorous with her anymore.

Most of the time, he drank too much to even think about it, although he still did occasionally. But the opportunities were rare. More often than not, when the kids were in bed, he was passed out in his chair downstairs. It was something Alice accepted. Their love life was yet another casualty of their life and broken years.

"Don't get sick again, Alice," he said, in the same tone he had used when he talked to her earlier on the couch, filled with tenderness and worry, and love for her.

"I won't. I promise." He nodded, and then turned over on his side, and went to sleep, snoring softly, as she watched him, wondering if life would ever be the same again. It seemed unlikely that it would.

Chapter Six

For the next few days Johnny came and went, going back and forth between his own house and the Adamses'. He seemed to be spending a lot of time watching Becky, and he looked unhappy late one afternoon when he came home to his mother.

"Where have you been?" She sounded like the mother of any teenager, and he laughed at the question when he walked in.

"I was at Becky's. The kids were all going wild and driving her crazy."

"I don't suppose you helped her with them," his mother teased.

"I would have if I could, Mom." He had always been good with them, and he liked them. "All I could do was keep an eye on them, and make sure none of them got a book of matches and burned down the house. They're a handful. She stayed home from work today to help her mom out. Two of them had the flu and couldn't go to school. But it sure isn't much of a life for Becky. She needs more than just that in her life. At least when I was around she got to go out and have some fun sometimes. She never goes anywhere now, Mom."

"I know. I keep telling Pam that. They both need to get out more."

"I'm not sure they can afford to," Johnny said honestly. But much as he hated to see her move on, he knew that Becky needed a boyfriend. There was nothing he could do about it, but he realized that at eighteen, she had a right to more than the life she was leading. Her siblings were as much her responsibility as her mother's. Sometimes more, because her mother worked longer hours. It saddened him that Becky never had fun anymore.

"I offered to baby-sit for her. Charlie could help me."

"If you can drag her off of the basket-ball court once in a while, which I doubt, sometime between basketball and baseball season. Why don't we try to get Dad to one of her games, Mom?"

"I have," she said unhappily. "He won't go. He never has. You know as well as I do, he thinks it's stupid for girls to play sports."

Johnny looked instantly annoyed. "She's a fantastic athlete, better than I was. He'd see that if he'd ever go to watch her."

"Well, he won't," Alice said, closing the subject. She had said it to Jim hundreds of times herself, but he said he wasn't going to waste his time, watching a bunch of girls play boys' sports, badly. It was useless to discuss it further with him, and Alice knew it. She had tried for years.

"He's the one who's missing out, as much as she is," Johnny said, looking frustrated.

"I go. That's something." But they both knew it wasn't what Charlotte wanted, or not all of it at least. She wanted her father's attention and approval, and so far she had never won it. Alice worried about what it would mean to her later, when she looked back and remembered that her father had never seen her win a single game, hit a home run, or win a trophy. And she had nearly as many as Johnny, including an award for MVP in the league for her last baseball season. Her picture had even been in the local paper. And Jim hadn't even mentioned it to her. But if Bobby had been able to play, he'd have noticed, and told all his friends.

Johnny came with her to pick Bobby up at school again that day, and he and his mother chatted all the way there in the car. And Bobby seemed in better spirits when he got in. He turned and stared straight at Johnny in the backseat, and then turned around and looked out the window as they drove home, and his mother chatted with him. She always acted as though she expected him to answer her, but wasn't upset when he didn't.

And once they got home, she gave him milk and cookies. Johnny had gone upstairs, back to his room, to put away his jacket. And a few minutes later, Bobby rushed upstairs, and Alice stayed in the kitchen to slice some vegetables for dinner. She had promised to make Charlotte's favorite dinner, of southern fried chicken, and mashed potatoes, with the zucchini fritters she loved.

Charlotte came home late that afternoon, and she went outside almost immediately to shoot some baskets, just as Johnny had done at her age, and after a while Alice was chilly, and went upstairs to get a sweater. She could hear sounds coming from Bobby's room. He was playing one of his talking tapes that she had bought for him, to inspire him, but the program had never worked. It had been a nice thought though. She poked her head into the room and blew him a

kiss, and she saw Johnny sitting on the
window seat, watching Bobby and saying nothing. And Alice winked at him,
before going back downstairs to the
kitchen. She had almost finished making
dinner when Johnny came back downstairs and looked longingly at a plate of
cookies. But no matter how normal he
looked to her, he could not eat them.
There were some things he didn't do,
and few he missed as much as her cookies and apple pie.

"Is Bobby okay?" she asked, looking
distracted, as she put the last touches on
the zucchini fritters.

"He's fine," Johnny said matter-of-
factly, as he hopped up on one of the
kitchen counters. He was swinging his
feet just the way Bobby would have.
"He sees me," he said, and then waited
for his mother's reaction to what he'd
said.

"Who sees you?" she asked, putting
something back in the refrigerator, and
taking something else out.

"Bobby," Johnny said, and then grinned as she came out of the refrigerator in rapid reverse, and stared at him.

"How do you know?"

"I can tell. Besides, he touched me," he said as though it were the most natural thing in the world.

"You let him? See you, I mean? Are you supposed to do that?"

"I don't know. I didn't think anyone could except you, Mom. But he does." He looked happy about it.

"Did you scare him?" she asked, looking worried.

"Of course not. Why would he be scared of me? Did he look scared to you when you walked into the room a few minutes ago?"

"No, he didn't." At least he couldn't tell anyone. Maybe that was why "they" had let Bobby see him too. "What did you tell him?"

"That I came back for a visit, and I can't stay. But I'll be here for a little while, pretty much what I told you. It's the truth. He was happy to see me.

God, I love him, Mom." Johnny had always been wonderful with him. He had been thirteen the summer Jim had had the accident with him, and Johnny had been devastated when he thought Bobby wouldn't survive. And forever after, he had been his great defender. "I talked to him for a long time about wanting to come to see him because I never said good-bye." Alice's eyes filled with tears as she listened, and then she smiled at the son she loved so much. She loved all her children, but she knew more than ever now how much she loved this one.

"It must have been you I heard when I went upstairs. I thought it was one of the tapes I bought him. You'd better watch out that Charlie and Dad don't hear you talking to him." If they could. He nodded then, as Bobby wandered into the kitchen. And he grinned broadly when he saw Johnny with his mom.

"This is pretty exciting, Bobby, isn't it?" she said softly, and he nodded, looking from one to the other. "But we can't tell anyone," not that he could have, or would have anyway. But it touched her heart to see that his eyes were dancing. "Do you suppose the whole family will get to see you eventually?" Alice asked Johnny. "We all missed you. Dad and Charlotte did too."

"Maybe they don't need to see me as badly as you two." But the truth was he didn't know the reason. He would have given anything if Becky could see him too, and she missed him desperately, but it was obvious she couldn't see him. "I don't know how this thing works, or why, Mom. It just does. We have to accept it. The rules are pretty stringent. I'm not supposed to scare anyone, make trouble for anyone, or complicate anyone's life. I'm here to fix things, that's all."

"Like what?" She was still curious about it, and Bobby was listening intently.

"I don't know yet. Just 'things.' You know, like you fixing dinner," he teased

her, and she grinned at him, just as they
heard Jim's car pull into the driveway.
She glanced out the window to make
sure it was him, and she could see Charlotte still shooting baskets outside. And
much to her chagrin, Alice saw Jim
walk right past Charlotte. She glanced at
her father, and the two never exchanged
a word. Alice turned back to her sons,
and Johnny hopped off the kitchen
counter, took Bobby's hand, led him out
of the kitchen, and up the stairs just as
their father walked in. And an instant
later, Alice heard them close the door
to Bobby's bedroom. Jim had already
opened the refrigerator and helped himself to a beer, and she thought he looked
exhausted.

"Hard day, dear?" she asked.

"No worse than usual," he said, as she
took their dinner out of the oven.
"How was yours?" he asked, without
much interest. He seemed particularly
distracted, and not in the mood to talk.

"Fine. Uneventful." She almost said,
"I was just talking to the boys when you

drove in," but of course she couldn't. Instead, she signaled to Charlotte outside, and ran upstairs to get Bobby. He and Johnny were sitting on the floor of his room, and she spoke to them in a whisper, turning first to her elder son. "Okay, time for you to go play, sweetheart. Bobby has to come down to dinner now."

"I could come too." Johnny looked a little hurt to be left out, even if he couldn't eat. "No one will see me, Mom."

"Bobby and I will, and what if we do something to give it away?" This was more than a little odd.

"Then everyone will think you're both crazy." Johnny laughed at her, and Bobby smiled one of his rare, wide smiles. With Johnny near at hand, he suddenly seemed far more expansive, and happier than he had been in months. "Okay, I'll go see Becky. I'll come home after dinner." It was just like having him alive again, ricocheting between the two houses. And he had a lot more time to spend with them, without school or work, or any obvious obligations. Whatever he had come here to "fix" was obviously not a full-time job. He was spending a lot of time with his mother and Bobby, and hanging around Becky. But Alice no longer needed to worry about him, she was just happy to have him there.

She took Bobby by the hand and led him downstairs, as Johnny followed close behind them, and they joined Charlotte and Jim in the kitchen. Charlie was telling him about the game they'd played that afternoon, and how well it had gone, and for once he showed a little interest, though not much. And a minute later, he interrupted her and told her about the trophy Johnny had won for basketball at her age.

"He was the best all-around athlete I've ever seen," Jim said proudly, and Johnny spoke loudly at him, although he couldn't hear.

"No, *she* is, Dad! Get with it!" But

neither of them heard him, as he waved at Bobby and his mother and walked out of the house through the front door. He opened and closed it so gently that no one heard him. And Bobby looked at his mother with wide eyes. They both knew that a miracle of sorts was happening to them, and the secret they shared seemed to bring them closer together than they'd ever been. She gently touched his shoulder as he took his seat between Charlotte and his dad.

It was an ordinary evening for them, and Johnny didn't come home until Alice was already in bed, reading.

"How was Becky?" his mother asked, peering at him over her reading glasses. She had just started to wear them, and Johnny said he liked them, which made her smile.

"She has a date tomorrow night," he said victoriously.

"How did that happen?" Alice looked stunned. They had just been talking about how sad her life was.

"She met a guy at work today. He's a

junior at UCLA, and he took a semester off to work for his father. He called tonight to ask her out." He sounded pleased as he told her, but he had mixed feelings about it. His name was Buzz and he was really handsome, and bright and nice. His father owned a chain of liquor stores, and he drove a Mercedes. He even liked kids, and had three brothers and two sisters himself. "I'm not sure he's good enough for her," Johnny told his mom, looking pensive. "But he looked okay to me when he walked into the drugstore. He went to the same high school we did. He recognized Becky as soon as he walked in. He graduated the year we were sophomores, and he always liked her, but he never asked her out before."

"Did you set that up for her?" his mother asked him with curiosity and admiration. It had been a nice thing for him to do, if he had, and he looked as though he felt good about it too.

"I think so," he said. He was not entirely sure yet of either his effect or his powers. "Charlie's still up, by the way. Isn't it kind of late for her?"

"Not really," his mother smiled. He was so grown-up now, in some ways, and still her little boy in others. "She's fourteen. You went to bed even later than that at her age," she said, amused by his policing his sister, just as she saw Jim walk into the room, looking tired. Neither of them had heard him come in, and he seemed more sober than he usually was at that hour.

"Who were you talking to?" he asked, looking straight at her.

"Oh . . . I . . . myself . . . I do that sometimes when I'm alone." She tried to look nonchalant.

"You'd better watch that," he teased her. "People are going to start saying funny things about you." She nodded, and Johnny left discreetly, and went to his own room. "You've been in awfully good spirits for the past few days. Any special reason?"

"Just feeling better, I guess. I think my ulcer's healing." And she didn't seem as consumed with grief as she had been. He had noticed that about her. He had noticed a number of things. The nice dinner she'd made for them that night, the easy way she talked to him. She didn't seem as agonized or as strained. The kids were in better shape too. He just wished that business was better. But at least their family seemed to be slowly on the mend, not that any of them would ever forget losing Johnny, or be the same again. Nor could he forgive himself for the accident he'd had with Bobby, and what the trauma of it had cost him. A lifetime of silence would serve to remind him of his own part in it, no matter how he might try to forget, or what methods he used to anesthetize himself.

They lay in bed and talked for a while that night, and she couldn't help wondering if he was drinking less, or just tolerating it better. It was hard to tell. And as though to confirm it, the next morning she found half the beers untouched in the six-pack next to his chair in the living room. She put them back in the refrigerator, just as Johnny came down the stairs in his varsity jacket. He had asked her to drive him to Pam's beauty school that morning. There was something he wanted to see there, and Alice had nothing else to do so she'd agreed to drive him. She loved driving him places, just the way she had when he was a little boy. She had always enjoyed the time they spent together in the car.

"What exactly am I supposed to say to Pam when we walk in?" Alice asked in the car as she drove him. He was playing with the radio, and switching from one station to the other, enjoying all his favorite music. He was having a ball.

"Boy, I really missed that," he said, looking happy, as she laughed, and reminded him that she had never visited Pam at work before, and she might find it a little odd. "Tell her you want to get your hair done."

"And then what? Why are we going there?"

"I'm not sure yet. There's someone I'm supposed to see. I figured it out last night. I'll tell you about it later," he said, putting the volume up so high that he could no longer hear her. And five minutes later, they were at the beauty school, and Pam looked startled to see Alice when she walked in.

"Are you okay?" She looked a little euphoric to Pam. Pam was beginning to wonder if they had put Alice on Prozac for her ulcer. She had been behaving just a little oddly, and she seemed strangely cheerful now all the time.

"I'm fine. I just thought it might be fun to get my hair done."

"Why? Are you going somewhere?"

"I'm going out to lunch afterward," Alice explained, trying to look normal, but feeling a little odd as she saw Johnny play with one of the dryers while she and Pam talked. "Don't play with that," Alice said, looking distracted, as Pam stared at her. She had no idea what Alice was talking about.

"Don't play with what?"

"I meant, don't play with my hair. Let's just do it."

"Sure, Alice, no problem," Pam said in a soothing tone. She was genuinely worried about her, but Alice looked fine, and she seemed to be in good spirits. Her ulcer was obviously getting better. But she was definitely a little strange these days.

Pam got one of the students to wash Alice's hair, and a few minutes later she assigned another student to give her a trim, and a third one was going to set it. And through it all, Johnny came and went with an official air. He looked very busy. And when he came back an hour later, his mother's hair was done, in a very stylish pageboy. And he had a man in tow. He was a rep from a line of hair products. He told Pam he was based in L.A., but had come to the area to introduce his products at local beauty salons and schools like this one. He was wearing a coat and tie, his hair was cut short, he looked respectable, and he was pleasant and interesting as he chatted

with Pam and Johnny's mother. Alice
thought he was very good looking, although Pam seemed not to notice. She
wasn't interested in meeting men. But
they were still talking when Alice left.
Pam had refused to let her pay for her
new hairdo and smiled as she waved
good-bye.

"Did you do that?" she asked her son,
and he feigned innocence.

"Do what?"

"Bring that guy in, with the line of
hair products. Did you have anything to
do with that, Johnny?"

"I have better things to do than fix
Becky's mom up with a blind date. That
is not why I came here," he said, looking dignified well beyond his years.

But Alice was not convinced. "I just
wondered."

Bobby smiled when he saw her hair,
when they picked him up at school that
afternoon. Johnny sat in the backseat
with him, and the radio was still blaring
on the way home, as Johnny sang to the
music, and Bobby nodded. He loved

having Johnny around again. Everything around him was always so full of life, and full of fun. As a child Bobby's age, Johnny had loved getting into mischief. And he was no different now. He was obviously having a good time being home, and visiting Bobby and his mother. So much so that when he went home, he took Bobby out to the backyard and shot some baskets with him. They were still out there when Charlotte came home, looking glum, having flunked her French test. But she smiled when she saw Bobby trying valiantly to sink a basket. She couldn't see her older brother, standing only inches away.

"Here, let me show you how," she said, taking the ball from him. She dribbled it a few times, and then sank it neatly on the first try, and showed her brother how she did it.

"Look at that, she's great!" Johnny said admiringly, as Bobby turned to look at him with a grin, and Charlotte watched them.

"Why are you looking behind me?"

Charlie asked him. "You have to keep your eye on the basket. Look at where you want to throw the ball, not over my shoulder."

"She's right," Johnny corrected him. "Stop looking at me, and do what she tells you. She's better at this than I am." Watching them from the window, Alice smiled to see all of her children standing under the basketball hoop together. She knew it might be the last time she'd ever see that. Knowing it made her sad, but seeing them there like that made her grateful for the moment. And she was still feeling the warmth of seeing them when Jim walked in half an hour later. He said he had something important to tell her.

"We got two new clients today," he said with a look of amazement. "They're both new businesses, and we're going to get a lot of work from them, to help them get set up. This could make a real difference to us."

"Really?" she said, looking pleased, and realizing suddenly what Johnny had

been up to all day. A man for Pam, po-
tentially, a date for Becky the night before, Charlotte seemed to be taking
Bobby under her wing. And Jim
had two new clients. Not bad for a
seventeen-year-old brand-new angel.

She complimented Johnny on all the
work he'd done, before he went up to
Bobby's room that night, after dinner.
He said he would be going out soon,
because he wanted to drop in on Becky.

"I just hope Buzz drives better than I
do," he said to his mother, and she
looked at him in horror.

"That's an awful thing to say," she
scolded him, and he smiled and bent to
kiss her before he left for the evening.
She stood in the kitchen for a minute
after he left, thinking about him. She
just hoped he didn't do his jobs too fast.
She was in no hurry for him to leave
them, and neither was he now.

Chapter Seven

Becky's first date with Buzz Watson went well, in spite of the fact that she talked about Johnny most of the evening. He took her to a movie, and out for a hamburger at Joe's Diner. It had been their destination the night Johnny had died, and everyone's favorite hangout while they were in school. And she told him about the years she and Johnny had spent going together all through high school. Johnny sat next to her for a while, listening to them, and he smiled at the memories she talked about. Listening to her, their time together seemed even more perfect now. She looked straight at him once or twice, but couldn't see him, and he somewhat grudgingly admitted to himself that Buzz was a nice guy. He had thought he was kind of stuck up when they were in school. He was one of the few "rich kids" who attended their high school, his father owned a successful chain of liquor stores all over southern California, his family went to Europe every summer, and he had always driven good cars.

Buzz was patient as he listened to Becky, and said that he had always thought Johnny was a great kid, although he didn't know him well. He didn't try to change the subject, or try to stop the flow of memories that tumbled from her like a waterfall. Her eyes filled with tears a couple of times, and when they did, Buzz gently took her hand.

He didn't get fresh with her on the drive home, and he told her about UCLA. He said he was going back the following semester, but his father had been sick that summer and had needed him to stay home to help at his stores. He was the oldest son, and had been working for his father for two months every summer, and during holidays and vacations ever since he was fourteen. He seemed to know a lot about the business, and chatted with her briefly about good wines, explaining some of their fine points to her. They went to France for a month every summer so his father could visit the vineyards, and he had learned a lot while he was there with him, more than the other kids, who, so far at least, weren't interested in his father's stores.

And he was obviously very taken with Becky. She was as pretty as he remembered her. He said he had once thought about inviting her to the prom, but knew he couldn't because of Johnny. He teased her about it, and said she didn't even know he was alive back then, which made her smile.

"Yes, I did. I just didn't think you liked me." She'd taken a French class

with him once, but his friends were two
years older than she was, and she'd been
pretty shy.

"I figured Johnny would kill me if I
asked you out," he said, laughing. "Besides, why would you have wanted me?
He was a football star." But there was a
lot about Buzz she liked now. He was
sensible, mature, intelligent, good looking, and he was more sophisticated and
grown up than Johnny had been. He
was nearly twenty-one, and to Becky he
was not so much a boy as a man. "I had
a good time tonight, Becky," he said
gently. "I know it must be hard for you
going out with someone else, after all
this time." Johnny was the only boy
she'd ever dated, the only one she'd ever
loved, but there was no changing the
fact that he was gone, and at some point,
she had to move on. She said she didn't
think she was ready to yet, but she had
enjoyed talking to Buzz all evening,
hearing about UCLA, his friends, his father's business, and the time he'd spent

in France. He liked kids too, and like
her, he had a lot of brothers and sisters.
He was the oldest of six, and she was the
oldest of five. Despite their different fi-
nancial circumstances, they had a lot in
common, and he asked if she'd like to
have dinner with him again, on Saturday night.

"I'd really like that, Buzz," she said
simply, as he helped her out of his car.
He was driving the Mercedes his father
had bought him when he left for UCLA
two years before. He had told her that
night that he was majoring in econom-
ics, and he was thinking about going to
graduate school and getting an M.B.A.
one day. And she had said she was going
to try for a scholarship again in the
spring, and hoped she could go to college in the fall. But in the meantime, she
was happy working at the drugstore,
and helping her mom with the other
kids. It was enough for now.

He suggested a French restaurant for
Saturday night that she'd heard of, but

never been to. Along with his knowledge of fine wines, he had a weakness for French food.

"How does that sound?" he asked, as he walked her to her front door. "Or would you rather just go to the drive-in and a movie? I thought maybe doing something different might be fun." It sounded like he could be happy either way. Johnny was leaning against a tree, listening to him while Buzz asked her, and he wanted to hate him for it. But somehow he couldn't pull it off, he was happy for Becky that Buzz wanted to spoil her a little bit. He couldn't even tell himself that Buzz was stuck up, because he wasn't, and it was obvious even to him that he liked Becky a lot. She turned and looked at Buzz solemnly as they reached her front door.

"I'm sorry I talked about Johnny a lot," she said softly, "I just miss him so much. Everything's so different now without him."

"It's okay," he said gently. "It's okay, Becky. I understand."

She nodded, and he held the front
door for her as they went in, and a
minute later he came out alone, and
drove away, as Johnny stood watching
the Mercedes disappear down the street,
and then turned slowly and went home.

His mother was in bed, reading, when
he got there, and she looked up at him
with a smile. "Where've you been all
night?" It was the same thing she would
have asked him any other night when
he came home, when he was alive.

"Out with Becky." As he said it, he
looked sad. And more like a boy than
a man.

"Didn't you tell me she had a date
tonight?" She looked puzzled, and she
could see that he was sad.

"Yeah. With Buzz Watson. He's kind
of a nice guy."

"Did you just follow them around all
night?" She looked worried as she asked
him. It didn't sound like a great idea to
her, or a happy circumstance for him,
even now.

"No. I just had dinner with them, and

then I did some other stuff, and I waited at the house while he dropped her off."

"Come over here," Alice said, patting the bed next to her, and he sat down. "Why did you do that?" She was concerned for her son, and the look in his eyes.

"I just wanted to make sure he was being nice to her."

"And was he?"

"Yeah. He let her talk about me all through dinner. He's taking her to Chez Jacques on Saturday night."

"Shouldn't you leave them alone for a while? It can't be much fun for you watching her go out with someone else. Why don't you stick around with me and Bobby on the nights she goes out?"

"I just thought I'd keep an eye on things in the beginning." He smiled at her then. "I guess that's kind of dumb, huh? I fixed her up with him, and now I'm not so sure I like it. This is hard, Mom." But not as hard as everything else they'd been through so far.

"What's happening with Pam?" Alice asked, trying to distract him.

Johnny smiled at her. "She's going out with Gavin, the guy from L.A., on Friday night. He's crazy about her."

"Good. She needs someone in her life. She hasn't even had a date since Mike died." Johnny nodded, looking pensive. He had a lot to think about, and a lot to do. But seeing Becky out with Buzz that night had pulled him back. He sighed then, and looked at his mother. He seemed more himself again.

"I'm okay, Mom. Everything's the way it should be. I'll go see Charlie for a while before I turn in. How was Dad tonight?"

"Asleep in front of the TV." She shrugged. It was the way things had been at their house every night for a long time. But at least lately he seemed a little better. And Alice was happier than she'd been in months. Johnny was home.

For the next few weeks, Buzz and

Becky spent a fair amount of time with each other. He took her to nice restaurants, hung out with her and her brothers and sisters, took her brothers to a football game, and brought her mom bottles of good wine to share with her new friend Gavin. Buzz was becoming a frequent visitor at the Adamses'. And so far, all Becky had done was hold Buzz's hand. He was moving slowly, he didn't want to rush her, and she was talking about Johnny a little less than she had at first. And they both liked the man who was visiting her mother every weekend from L.A. It was clear to all of them that he liked her a lot, and was crazy about her kids.

The four of them even went out to dinner one night, Gavin, Pam, Buzz, and Becky. They went to a little Italian restaurant, and Buzz suggested a terrific little-known Napa Valley wine. The foursome had a good time together, and Johnny was in good spirits when he came home that night, and described the entire evening to his mother.

"I still think you ought to take the night off when they go out," she chided him, and then asked him if he was going trick-or-treating with Bobby. She had been trying to figure out a costume for him. Charlotte had already announced that she was too old to go trick-or-treating that year, and she was going to stay home and hand out candy at the door with a group of friends. Alice was planning to walk Bobby around the neighborhood. And she was torn between dressing him up as Superman, Batman, or in a cute ninja costume she'd just seen.

"I'll go with him, Mom," Johnny volunteered.

"That would be fun. See if you can figure out what he'd want to be." She had dressed him as Luke Skywalker from *Star Wars* the previous year.

She was still mulling it over a few days later, when she walked past the door to Bobby's room after he got home from school. It was a chilly day, and she had come upstairs to get a sweater. She knew Charlotte was doing homework in her room, but she could hear voices coming from Bobby's. She assumed it was one of his talking tapes and smiled when she heard Johnny talking to him. Bobby couldn't answer, but at least he could hear and see him. She could hear both voices in the room, the talking tape and Johnny's. And as she walked toward her own room, she suddenly heard the sound of laughter. She stopped, and turned around, walked slowly to the door of Bobby's room, and listened. At first, all she could hear was Johnny, talking to him. She could no longer hear the tape, but she very distinctly heard a second voice, talking to him. And without thinking, she turned the knob, opened the door, and looked at both of them. Both boys were sitting on the floor, and Bobby's toys were spread all around them, as they glanced up at her in surprise and confusion.

"What are you two up to?" she asked casually, as she stepped into the room, and closed the door behind her, so no

one else would hear them. "Making a
mess? Or just having fun?" Her eyes
searched both her sons', sensing that
they shared a secret. Her heart trembled
as she looked at them, and Johnny
smiled oddly at her. "Is there something
funny going on here?" She looked from
one to the other, and Johnny looked
pointedly at his younger brother, and
then whispered something to him, as
she watched them.

Bobby raised his eyes slowly to hers,
and she felt as though an arrow were
piercing through her. She could barely
breathe, as she reached a hand out to
him, and then sat down next to them.
She didn't know why, but she wanted to
be closer to them, and she touched
Bobby's face with both her hands, as
tears filled her eyes for no reason she
could fathom. It was as though she
could feel something in him, something
that wanted to be free now.

"Are you okay?" she asked breath-
lessly, and the small child nodded, as
Johnny never took his eyes from him.

"Go on," Johnny said, as Bobby looked from his brother to his mother.

"Hi, Mom," Bobby whispered, as a sob broke from her, and she pulled him to her with such force that it left them both breathless, and then she pulled slowly away from him and looked down at him, laughing and crying, as she reached a hand out to Johnny and pulled him toward them.

"Hi, Bobby" was all she could answer at first. "I love you so much. . . . How long have you been talking?"

"Since Johnny came. He said I had to. We can't play any good games if I don't talk to him." Johnny was smiling at both of them, as Alice tried to wipe the tears from her cheeks, but they wouldn't stop coming.

"Will you talk to all of us now?" She couldn't help wondering for how long he had been capable of it, or thinking how much it would mean to his father. But as she asked him, Bobby shook his head and looked at Johnny.

"Maybe soon, Mom," Johnny said

quietly. "We need to do this one step at a time. Bobby wants to get used to talking to you first. But he's doing real well," he said, tousling Bobby's hair, "he said a real good word to me this morning." Bobby giggled at the memory of the word he had dared to say to his older brother. It was one he knew he wouldn't be allowed to use, even once he started talking, no matter how grateful they were to hear his voice.

"Can't we tell Daddy?" Alice felt terrible not sharing the news with him. She knew it would make all the difference in the world to him.

"Not yet," Johnny answered for him. "But soon, I promise." She didn't want to push either of them, but she was sorry not to tell Jim what had happened. But she somehow felt that it was best to respect Johnny's wishes.

They sat on the floor together for a long time, talking softly so no one would hear, and after a while, Charlotte knocked on the door and stuck her head in.

"Mom, your cookies are burning," she said matter-of-factly, seeing neither her older brother, nor the look of joy in her mother's eyes. All she saw was her mom on the floor, talking to Bobby, with his toys all around them. "I took them out of the oven," she said, and closed the door again, as Alice stood up and kissed both her sons before she left them. She went downstairs with a lighter step than she'd had in years, and all she could think of was how Jim would feel once he knew that Bobby was talking.

Her eyes went to Bobby's often at dinner that night, and he smiled as he looked at her. They had a huge secret to share, two of them, one that he could talk, and the other that Johnny had come back to them. It formed a bond between Alice and her youngest child that they had never shared before, and he stayed in the kitchen with her for a long time that night, after they finished dinner. He said nothing to her, but she could feel his heart tucked into her own, as he helped her clean up, and when they finished, she stopped and pulled her to him. "I love you, Bobby," she whispered to him. His arms held her tightly around her waist, and when she stepped back from him, he smiled at her, and went silently upstairs with Johnny.

Chapter Eight

Thanksgiving was painful for them that year, particularly for Jim and Charlotte. Alice felt sorry for both of them, and wished that she could have shared Johnny's presence with them. He hung around between Bobby and her part of the time, and made yummy faces as he stood over the turkey, while she was carving it in the kitchen. Jim had had enough to drink by then that she didn't trust him with it, or the carving knife. She didn't want him to destroy the bird, or hurt himself.

"Boy, that smells great, Mom. It's bigger than last year," Johnny said with admiration.

"I couldn't find one smaller than this,"

she said out loud to him, wrestling with one of the drumsticks, and then licking her fingers while Johnny sniffed at the gravy. "Be careful you don't spill that."

"Spill what?" Charlotte asked, looking blank, as she walked into the kitchen to help her.

"The gravy. Not you, I was talking to . . ." She was distracted and forgot that Charlotte couldn't see Johnny standing next to her.

"Who were you talking to, Mom?" Charlotte asked, looking worried.

"No one, sweetheart. I was just thinking out loud." Charlotte looked crestfallen as she walked out, carrying a platter of sweet potatoes with marshmallows on them. Her mother was clearly out of her mind with grief, and her father was already drunk halfway through the afternoon. Johnny was gone, and she wished they didn't have to celebrate at all, as she went back to the kitchen to get the cranberry jelly. Her mother had her back to her when she walked into the room, and had just said clearly "Stop that!" Charlotte thought she was definitely crazy. "If you touch one more thing, I'm going to kill you!" Alice said, sounding good-humored.

"I thought you wanted this stuff put on the table," Charlotte said as her mother turned around to look at her, and then blushed.

"Yes, I did. I'm sorry. . . . I get a little frazzled with all this cooking."

"Mom, you've got to stop talking to yourself like that," Charlie said, looking nervous. She'd been doing it for two months. Charlotte knew why, it was because of Johnny's death of course, but it just didn't seem normal or healthy. Even her father had noticed, but he never said anything to Alice about it. He had told Charlotte she always talked to herself now when she was alone in their bedroom. He had walked in several times when she was having a full-blown conversation with herself. "Mom, are you okay?" Charlotte asked her, as she juggled the cranberry jelly in one hand and the string beans in the other.

"I'm fine, dear. Honest. I'll be out in two minutes with the turkey."

"Okay, now go play while we eat," she told Johnny in a whisper before leaving him in the kitchen, and hurrying into the other room with the turkey.

"I can't miss Thanksgiving, Mom." He looked hurt at the suggestion.

"You'll make Bobby act funny . . . and I'll wind up saying something I shouldn't," she whispered to him.

"I'll be good. I promise," he said solemnly, and then followed her in as she carried the stuffing and the carved turkey. Thanksgiving had always been his favorite holiday next to Christmas.

Alice served everyone, and Jim looked vague as he dug into his dinner. Charlotte said nothing, and Bobby smiled when he glanced up at Johnny. But Johnny put a careful finger to his lips and warned him not to look at him, which made Alice giggle.

"Whass so funny?" Jim asked, slurring his words. And Alice looked at him sadly. It was painful to see him that way, not only for her, but for the children. Bobby glanced at him with disappointment, and shook his head.

"Why did Dad have to get so drunk today?" Johnny asked her when she went back to the kitchen to carve more turkey for them.

"Why do you think?" she said with a sigh, putting more dressing on the platter. "Because we all miss you. And all the usual old stuff. It's a shame he can't see you too. I think it would help him so much. Why do you suppose they wouldn't let him see you, like me and Bobby?"

"Because he wouldn't understand it, Mom," Johnny said without hesitation.

"I'm not sure I do either. But I sure do love it," she said, stopping to kiss him, and then she walked back into the other room with seconds for Jim and the children.

"Talking to yourself again?" Jim asked

her with a look of concern. Even after drinking too much, he could hear her talking to herself.

"Sorry," she said, as Charlotte looked up at her miserably. She hated it when her father got drunk. And now her mother was acting crazy too. Thanksgiving without Johnny was agonizing. It seemed unfair to Alice that Charlotte couldn't see him too. But maybe she wouldn't have understood it either. Whatever the reason, she couldn't see him. He stood right next to her for part of the meal, so close that she should have been able to sense something, but she didn't. "The Adamses said they'd come by after they eat their turkey," Alice said to everyone at the table.

"Why do they have to come here?" Jim didn't sound pleased about it. He just wanted to finish eating, and sit in front of the TV, drinking beer, and watching football.

"They're our friends, Jim," Alice chided.

"So what? Johnny's gone, and Becky's

not his girlfriend." Alice said nothing, and they all went on eating, and a few minutes later, Charlotte helped her clear the table. It was a relief to end the meal and move around the kitchen.

"I hate him," Charlotte said, as she set the platters down on the counter. Bobby came in with his plate, and his mother took it from him. Jim had already abandoned the table, without waiting for the pumpkin pie or the whipped cream she had made for it.

"He can't help it, Charlie. You know that," her mother said gently.

"Yes, he can. He doesn't have to get drunk all the time. It's disgusting." Charlotte looked heartbroken, and it pained Alice to see it.

"He misses Johnny," Alice said, knowing full well that he also felt guilty about Bobby, and had since he'd stopped speaking.

"I miss him too," Charlotte said practically, "so do you. You're not falling-down drunk," she said with a grim expression. "All you do is talk to yourself. That's pretty weird, but at least it's not as sick as what he does."

"Don't say things like that about your father," Alice said firmly.

"Why not? It's true. Dad's a drunk, Johnny's gone. Bobby is never going to talk again." Her eyes filled with tears as she listed the miseries that afflicted all of them, but only some of them were true. Bobby had begun to talk again, and Johnny was back, for a while at least. And she was talking to him, not herself.

"Maybe Dad will stop drinking one of these days," Alice said with a sigh, as she cut wedges of the pumpkin pie, but no one was hungry. "People do, you know."

"Yeah, sure," she said, unconvinced, helping herself to a dollop of whipped cream with her finger. "I'll believe that when I see it."

"He's been better lately," Alice said hopefully, but Charlotte didn't look as though she agreed with her.

"Not today. He could have at least stayed sober on Thanksgiving."

The three of them picked at their pumpkin pie, and Johnny sat at the table in his father's empty seat between Charlotte and Bobby. And as Alice started clearing the table, the doorbell rang, it was Becky and her mother and brothers and sisters. They made a noisy entrance, as Johnny sat, staring at Becky. She looked beautiful in a dark blue velvet dress, with her shining gold hair hanging down her back just the way he had loved it. Alice felt a pang of sorrow for him as she saw the way he watched her.

"Happy Thanksgiving, everyone!" Pam said as she handed Alice an apple pie she and Becky had made that morning. "How was dinner?"

"It was all right," Alice said quietly, as Charlotte took Becky and the girls up to her room, and Johnny silently followed. Alice then suggested that Bobby take the boys up to his room, and Pam followed her into the kitchen. She could see easily that it had been a hard Thanksgiving for them, and she remembered all too well how hard it had been for them the first year after Mike died. All of the holidays had been agony for them, and it was obvious that this one was no different. At their house, Becky had cried on and off all through dinner, and talked about how much she missed Johnny.

"Where's Jim?" Pam asked, as Alice nodded toward the living room. They could hear the TV blaring.

"He's watching football. He's not in such great shape either. I guess no one is." Even though she and Bobby could see Johnny, it was painful knowing how much the others felt his absence.

"The holidays are tough the first year. Christmas will be even worse. Start bracing yourself for it." Alice nodded in answer, and continued rinsing the dishes.

"How's your life?" Alice asked. She had put a pot of coffee on, and Pam poured them each a cup when it was ready.

"Interesting," she confessed with a sheepish grin. "I'm not sure what's happening, or what it means, but I think I like it. I'm still seeing Gavin, and I really like him."

"I'm happy for you," Alice said, sitting down at the kitchen table with her finally, once all the dishes were in the dishwasher. It was nice for both of them, having someone to talk to.

"He's great with the kids, and he's nice to me. It's been so long since I've gone anywhere, or done anything. He takes me out to dinner every Saturday. It probably doesn't mean anything, but he's good company, and it's nice to have an excuse to get dressed and have my hair done. It's fun to be more than just a mom for a change, and a chauffeur. He even plays baseball with the boys on Sunday mornings." What Pam said made Alice wonder if she let him stay over, and Pam laughed as she saw her friend's expression. "He stays with a friend here." They both laughed then, and chatted for a long time at the kitchen table, and then they finally went upstairs to check on their children.

The Adams girls were sitting on
Charlotte's bed and the floor of her
room, talking about boys and school,
and Becky said something about Buzz
to Charlotte. And as they chatted,
Johnny was sitting at Charlotte's desk
and smiling. He couldn't take his eyes
off Becky. And from the doorway, Alice
smiled at him. During his entire lifetime, she couldn't have paid him to sit in
on a session like this one. But it was different now, and he loved being close to
Becky. It was as though he wanted to
drink her in, and just enjoy watching
her. It seemed like he was storing one
more memory to take with him.

Pam and Alice went to Bobby's room
then, and Peter and Mark were tossing
around one of his baseballs. Alice suggested they go outside and toss the ball
around and shoot some baskets, and
when they got up to go, Bobby silently
followed. He liked being with them.
And then the two women went downstairs again. They passed Jim sound
asleep in front of the TV, with four

empty beer bottles next to him. Green Bay had just scored a touchdown, and he was snoring loudly.

"How is he?" Pam whispered, as they took refuge in the kitchen, and Alice glanced out the window at their children. And this time she saw that Johnny was with them. Bobby was quietly standing next to him, as the Adams boys started shooting baskets.

"Not so great, I guess," Alice said about her husband. "He seemed better for a while, but the past few days haven't been terrific."

"It's the holidays," Pam said wisely. "It'll probably be like this for all of you till after Christmas." Alice nodded in answer, and they went on talking for another hour about the beauty school, and Gavin, and then Pam finally stood up, and said she was going to collect her troops and go home, but it took them another half-hour to do it. And as they left, Johnny stood watching them from the doorway, and then came to talk to his mother in the kitchen.

"She looked pretty, didn't she, Mom?" He was talking about Becky, and his mother nodded. "She says she really likes Buzz. I'm happy for her," he said honestly, but it was obvious that it wasn't easy for him. Letting go of Becky was one of the hardest things he had to do now, but he knew she had to have a life without him. He could offer her nothing. She couldn't even see him, unlike Bobby and his mother. He had no way of reaching out to Becky, except through his heart, and wishing her a happy future.

"I know she misses you," Alice said kindly. "It's as hard for her as it is for you." She wanted to say they'd both get over it in time, and she knew they would, but somehow it didn't seem right to say it. "I'd better go wake Dad up," she said with a sigh then, and Johnny nodded.

"I'll check on Bobby," Johnny volunteered, and then he turned, remembering something. "Are you going to Charlotte's game tomorrow?" She was playing basketball for her school, and the game was a big one.

"I thought we all would," Alice said, turning off the lights in the kitchen.

"Dad too?" Johnny said, smiling. He was happy to hear it.

"No, he can't. He's working," she said without expression.

"He doesn't have to work the day after Thanksgiving, Mom. He could come if he wanted." But he never went to Charlotte's games, never had, and had no interest in them. According to him, girls were never great athletes. But he was dead wrong on this one. Charlotte was a star, even more so than he had been.

"I'll ask him," Alice promised, more to mollify her son than because she thought Jim would do it. And then Johnny went upstairs to see his brother, and she walked into the living room, and gently shook her husband. He stirred after a minute, snorted loudly, and then squinted at her.

"What time is it?" He wasn't sure if it was night or morning.

"It's after ten. Let's go up to bed." He nodded and stood up unsteadily. He could hardly make it up the stairs, and it made her heart ache to see it. "I'll come in in a minute," she said, and then went to check on Bobby. He was in bed, and Johnny was reading to him, lying next to him, their heads on the pillow side by side. Both boys looked up at her and grinned. For them at least, it was the perfect Thanksgiving. "Good night, you two," she whispered. "I love you," she said, as she stooped over them and kissed them. "Don't let Bobby stay up too late," she warned, and Bobby snuggled up happily next to his brother, as she gently closed the door behind her, and walked across the hall to see Charlotte. She was lying on her bed and staring up at the ceiling. "Are you okay, sweetheart?" Alice asked, looking concerned, and sat down next to her on the bed. It was easy to see that she was upset about something.

"Yeah. Sort of. It's weird hearing Becky talk about her new boyfriend. I think she really likes him." But it made Charlie miss Johnny more.

"That's nice for her," Alice said, and meant it. "She can't mourn Johnny forever, Charlie. It wouldn't be right. And her mom says he's really good to her. Johnny would like that. What about your game tomorrow? Are you all set for that?" Charlotte nodded, but looked unenthusiastic.

"Dad never missed any of Johnny's games," she said in a monotone. It wasn't an accusation, just a statement. And year for year, she had won more trophies than he had at her age. "Are you coming to it, Mom?"

"I wouldn't miss it for the world," her mother leaned over and kissed her. "I'll bring Bobby." Charlotte nodded and said nothing. As much as she loved her mother, it would have meant the world to her if her father had come, just once. If he cared enough to do that. But they both knew he didn't. She wasn't Johnny.

Alice didn't say anything about it to Jim that night. There was no point. He was already asleep by the time she got to bed, drunk on beer and wine, and too much turkey. But in the morning, she said something to him over breakfast.

"Girls can't play basketball," he said decisively in answer as he drank his second cup of coffee. "You know that."

"You never missed any of Johnny's games," she said, annoyed at the way he had said it.

"That was different."

"Was it? Why? Because he was a boy?"

"He was a great athlete," Jim said matter-of-factly. He had a splitting headache.

"So is Charlotte. Maybe even better than he was. Johnny always said that about her."

"He was just trying to make her feel good."

"Why don't you come and see for yourself?" she asked him, as Johnny and Bobby walked into the kitchen. Bobby said nothing, as usual. And Johnny stopped to kiss his mother, but Jim couldn't see that. "You could still get in plenty of time at the office. The game doesn't start until four o'clock, in the gym at her school. I think it would mean a lot to her if you would be there. Johnny always went. And you know a lot more about the game than I do. I think it's important that you be there."

"Oh come on, Alice. Don't be silly. She won't even know the difference."

"Yes, she will," Alice persisted, as Johnny sat down at the table, next to his father, staring at him intently. "Why don't you think about it?" Alice said, as she set a bowl of cereal down in front of Bobby. Jim seemed not to see him. To him, Bobby was as invisible as Johnny was to him. Ever since Bobby had stopped speaking, his father had ignored him. Acknowledging him, and the reason why he could no longer talk, was just too painful for him.

"I've got a lot of work to catch up on, for my new clients. I'm going to be working all weekend." But at least that

was good for him, and she was aware
that his business was slowly improving.
She kept hoping that if he felt better
about his work, he might stop drinking,
or slow down at least. He had been better since Johnny had come, but there
was still a lot of room for improvement.

He left for work a few minutes later,
and both boys disappeared outside
somewhere. Alice was alone in the
kitchen when Charlotte came down for
breakfast, and she left a few minutes
after that for practice. At least she
seemed in better spirits, and she said
nothing at all about her father. She
wasn't expecting him to come, and
Alice didn't tell her she had talked to
him about it, and gotten nowhere.

And at a quarter to four, she and
Bobby got into the front seat of her car,
and Johnny got in the backseat behind
them. He was talking animatedly about
the game, and Bobby was talking and
laughing with his brother, as Alice
smiled and listened to them. It was like

a dream come true, being with them, listening to Bobby talk, and having Johnny back with them.

She didn't know how long he would be with them, but it was a gift beyond any she could have hoped for. And by the time they arrived at the high school, they were in great spirits, and looking forward to the game.

The game went well for Charlotte's team. The score was 26 to 15 by the middle of the second quarter, and Bobby was hopping up and down in his seat, clapping for Charlotte. She scored another three-pointer, and Johnny went crazy watching her. He couldn't believe how well she was playing. And then, as they waited for the second half to start, Alice saw a familiar form out of the corner of her eye, and turned to see her husband making his way across the gym, looking somewhat tentative, but smiling at them.

"I can't believe it," she whispered, as Bobby stared, and Johnny gave a victorious whoop. Alice almost cried when she saw Charlotte's expression when she saw her father. It was the first game he had come to. "How did you manage that?" she whispered to Johnny, just before Jim reached them.

"To be honest with you, I'm not sure," Johnny said to his mother. "I've been thinking about it a lot, and wishing for it ever since we got here. Maybe he heard me, or felt it, or something." Johnny still wasn't aware of how he influenced things, yet he was beginning to realize that when he thought of something hard enough, it happened. It was a miraculous kind of power that seemed to flow through him. And suggesting something to someone's thought invariably seemed to make them want to do it.

Jim had reached them by then, and sat down between his wife and Bobby, but said nothing to the child. His eyes were riveted on Charlotte. Suddenly, he seemed very intent on her playing, as though he had never before seen it.

"She's playing incredibly," Alice said proudly, and he nodded.

And she scored another basket as soon as the clock started. Jim said nothing, he just watched her. But she scored another three points with an amazing shot in the last two minutes of the game, and everyone cheered her. Her team had slaughtered their opponents, and twenty of the winning points had been Charlotte's. The rest of the team carried her around on their shoulders, when the game was over. And when Alice turned to him, she saw that Jim was smiling broadly. She couldn't even remember the last time she'd seen him look that happy. He was immensely proud of his daughter, as though he were seeing her for the very first time and finally discovering her talent.

"That was a hell of a game, wasn't it?" he said to Alice, and she nodded, as tears stung her eyes. And a few minutes later Charlotte joined them, looking happy and excited to see her father.

"Thanks for coming, Dad," she said shyly.

"You did a great job, Charlie," he

said, standing up and putting an arm around her shoulders. "I was really proud of you!" he said gruffly, as he shook her gently like a bear playing with a cub, proud of some new achievement of his offspring.

They followed her out of the gym, after she had changed, and she couldn't see him, but Johnny had his arm around her, and she looked pensive as she silently thought about him.

"You know, Johnny played a game like that once," her father reminisced as they drove home, "he won a trophy for it."

"I think we have a good chance to be in the division finals this year," she said with a look of gratitude for his interest. It was all so new to her, but she was reveling in it.

"If you do, I'll come see them," Jim promised. He had been vastly impressed by the game he'd just seen her play. She had real athletic talent. More than he'd ever dreamed.

They stopped to buy groceries on the

way home, and by the time they got back, it was time to start dinner. Alice busied herself in the kitchen, and Bobby went outside to shoot baskets with Charlotte, as their father watched them and coached Charlotte, and Johnny went along to watch them. A few minutes later, he walked back into the kitchen, to talk to his mother.

"That was pretty cool of Dad to come, wasn't it?" he said, sounding as pleased as he felt. He knew what it had meant to Charlie. Even their father had seemed to "get it." And he had been blown away by the way Charlie played. He was already talking about going to the next game.

"I think you have more power than you think," Alice said softly, so no one else would hear her. "What you do has an effect on all of us. . . . Look at Bobby. And Dad going to the game. It's like magic." His gentle, loving touch was improving all their lives, one by one.

"Bobby was just ready, Mom. Five years is a long time not to talk." She knew it all too well. Jim had been drinking heavily on a daily basis ever since Bobby had become silent.

"When are we going to tell Dad about Bobby talking?" Alice asked. She had been wondering about it ever since she had discovered their secret, and hoped it would be soon. She knew just how much it would mean to Jim.

"Not yet," Johnny answered. "Bobby's not ready. But he will be, soon, I hope. We still have a few twists and turns in the road here."

"What does that mean?" She looked puzzled.

"To tell you the truth, I'm not sure, Mom. I just feel things. I don't know why, and I'm never sure how they're going to work out. I just think things, and they come, kind of on their own. But they happen the way I thought. But I do know that Bobby needs to practice talking a little bit, and he has to be prepared to tell Dad." Alice knew what a gift of freedom it would be for Jim, it would free him from the guilt, and it might change his life, and theirs, to know that Bobby could talk again. She was anxious for that to happen. But Johnny insisted it was too soon to tell him, and she somehow knew she had to respect that, and so did Bobby. Johnny seemed to know what he was doing. The results were good so far. For the moment, only their mother could share their conversations with them. Johnny wanted their victories to be more solid, he didn't want Bobby to feel like he failed if anything went wrong, or to be so nervous, he stumbled when he talked.

She had dinner on the table for them half an hour later, and Jim talked at length to Charlotte about the game, and how she could score even more points if she tightened up her game. The suggestions he made were good ones, and Charlotte was momentarily impressed. It was all she had ever wanted from him. A door had finally opened between them, and her father had taken a giant step into her world. The love and approval she had always wanted from him was finally hers.

"I'll try, Dad," she said, excited about the attention he was giving her, and glowing from it. It was almost like the conversations he used to have with Johnny. He was suddenly respectful of her, and he could see how well she played. And he had to admit for once, she was a damn fine little athlete. His approval shone in his eyes, and listening to him, Charlotte looked like she had been given the Hope diamond. She was the happiest girl in the world.

The next day, after Jim came home from work, he offered to take her out for a soda at the drive-in, and for once it didn't seem like he had been drinking before he got home. Alice smiled as they left, and Charlotte hurried out to the car with her father. She asked him a number of questions about the sports he'd played as a young man, as he turned the key in the ignition. And a moment later, Alice saw them drive off, and she went outside to watch Johnny shoot baskets with Bobby. What they had just seen was like a miracle to them. It seemed as though Jim had never paid a moment's attention to Charlotte, but he was making up for lost time now.

Alice waited for them to return before starting dinner, but she was startled when she glanced at the clock, and saw that it was after seven. They should have been home long before. They had been gone for nearly two hours, and at eight o'clock she was panicked. But she was even more so, when the hospital called her at eight-thirty. They said that Charlotte and Jim were there, they were both fine, except that Charlotte had a mild concussion.

"What happened?" Alice was horrified as she listened to the voice on the phone explain it to her. They had had a minor accident in the car. Jim had hit a parked truck, but had suffered no injuries. Charlotte's head had hit the dashboard, and after they watched her for a while, they were going to send her home with her father. And as soon as she hung up, Alice told Johnny about it. She had long since fed Bobby a sandwich, and afterward he had gone to his room to do some homework. So she didn't have to worry about frightening him when she told Johnny about the accident. And he whistled long and hard when she told him about it.

"Was he drinking, Mom?" Johnny asked her, and she looked confused.

"I don't know. He seemed okay when he left," she said honestly. But they both knew that he might have stopped somewhere for a couple of beers or more. He could have gotten just drunk enough to hit another car. And at that exact moment, Alice knew she'd had enough. He had just endangered a child for a second time. The risk he presented while drinking was suddenly intolerable to her.

She was still angry at herself, and at him, when Jim came home with Charlotte two hours later. She was too angry to even speak to him. All they had told Charlotte to do was rest and take it easy for a few days. They thought she could be playing basketball again the following weekend. But that was beside the point to Alice. She knew Charlotte could have been killed.

The look on Jim's face, when he walked in, told its own story. He was ashen. He said nothing to his wife, but poured himself a cup of coffee, and looked long and hard at her, trying to gauge her reaction, when she came downstairs after putting Charlotte to bed. Alice was livid, as Johnny quietly withdrew and went back upstairs to Bobby. He'd been waiting in the kitchen with his mother when Charlotte and Jim came home. "Do you realize you could have killed her?" she said furiously. He didn't answer. They both knew the consequences of accidents like the one he'd just had with Charlotte. "I'm not going to let you drive the kids anymore, if you can't be responsible," she said, looking angrily at him. "You can drink all you want, but don't get in a car with my children," she said firmly, and he sat down at the kitchen table, looking like a beaten man. He had scared himself, and Charlotte, to death.

"I know, you have every right to say that, and to be very angry with me." If there was one thing they both knew, it was the price of accidents like the one he'd just had. They had lived through it all too vividly with Bobby. Jim himself had never recovered from it, nor had their son.

"I'm never going to be able to forgive you, and neither are you, if you have another accident with one of our kids," Alice said, looking right at him, and he had tears in his eyes when he turned away from her.

"Look. I get it. I feel awful. You don't have to say anything, Alice. I said it all to myself after it happened." And she could see that he meant it. "I just had a couple of beers before we came home."

"I'm going to say a lot, Jim, if you do it again. If you drink, don't drive our kids. If you do, I'm going to leave and take them with me." She had never said anything like that to him before.

"Are you serious?" He looked horrified by what she was saying. He could see that she meant it. Something in her had snapped when the hospital called.

"Look," Jim insisted, "I told you it won't happen again." She gave him a long hard look, and then silently walked out of the kitchen, went upstairs to their bedroom, and closed the door.

Jim came up a few minutes later, and said nothing to her. Alice was already in bed, and in no mood to talk to him. And as he slipped quietly into bed and turned off the light, Alice could hear Johnny and Bobby moving around in the next room. But Jim was so exhausted from the emotions of the evening, he seemed to hear nothing, and within minutes, he was asleep.

Chapter Nine

The tension in the house the day after Jim and Charlotte's accident hung over them like cement. Neither Jim nor Alice spoke at the breakfast table, Bobby was silent as usual, and Charlotte was in bed, asleep. And after Alice cleared the dishes, Jim stood watching her for a minute, trying to get up the courage to talk to her. But it was obvious she didn't want to talk to him.

"I'm going to the office today," he said, as though expecting a reaction from her, but he got none. She turned around and looked at him in silence. "Will you be all right here with the kids? I mean, with Charlotte and everything. . . ." His voice drifted off as he saw the pain and accusation in her eyes. It was obvious that she felt he had betrayed her. "Look, dammit, I didn't do it on purpose."

"You didn't need to drink when you took her out. You could have waited till you got home."

"I know," he said in a choked voice. "I was excited about the game. She's going to be all right, Alice. I didn't kill her." He tried to defend himself, but it was futile. They both knew he was wrong.

"If you want to risk yourself, I don't like it, but that's your choice. You have no right to make those kinds of decisions with our children." What it told her was that she could no longer trust him with their children. Neither his driving nor his judgment could be relied on anymore.

"I won't do it again," he said weakly, feeling rotten. He hated knowing that he had upset her, and Charlotte had gotten hurt.

"No, you won't," she said with a different tone than he'd ever heard before, "because I won't let you." He said nothing, and a few minutes later, he left, and Johnny walked into the kitchen and looked at his mother's face with concern.

"I hate it when you guys fight," he said sadly.

"Do you blame me? He could have killed your sister."

"Maybe this time it'll teach him a lesson." But if he hadn't learned the lesson five years before, when Bobby nearly drowned, Alice was beginning to think he never would. Maybe his drinking was now a permanent part of their existence, and there was no hope that he would change it. For the first time, the night before, she had begun to accept that. And she didn't like what it meant for their future. She had always thought he would stop drinking eventually, or cut down dramatically, but he never had. If anything, he'd gotten worse over the years, since Bobby's accident. They had lost Johnny, and she had no intention of losing either of the others. Or him, if he decided to drive while he was drunk. "I'm sorry, Mom," Johnny said sadly. It pained him to see her so worried.

She went upstairs to check on Charlotte then, and after a while, she came back downstairs to cook her breakfast. And Pam came over to visit her that afternoon. She had a date again that night with Gavin, and she had dropped in just to say hi, and was horrified when Alice told her what had happened to Charlotte.

Alice was still upset when Pam arrived, but she didn't tell her she had threatened to leave Jim over it. They talked for a while, and when Pam left, Alice took Bobby out for an ice cream, and then came home to fix dinner. And at seven, Jim still wasn't home, and she called him at the office. But he wasn't there either. She assumed he was on his way home, but an hour later, he was still out, and she was frantic. She couldn't help wondering if he had lied to her, not gone to the office at all, and was seeing someone on the side, or perhaps he was too drunk to come home. She had never suspected him of cheating on her before, but there was no telling what he might do, she realized now, when he'd been drinking. It felt as though their life had sunk to a new low.

He came in at eight-fifteen, looking nervous and uncomfortable, and he seemed surprised to see Bobby and Alice eating dinner at the kitchen table. She glanced up at him without a word, but she could see in an instant that he was cold sober.

"I'm sorry. I didn't realize how late it was," he said awkwardly. "I just left the office. I had to catch up on some work." You could have cut the tension between them with a knife.

"I called you over an hour ago," she said, with eyes filled with accusation. She was still angry at him from the night before, and this added fuel to the fire.

"I had to stop somewhere on the way

home. I said I was sorry," Jim said, and she didn't answer him, but put dinner on a plate for him, as Bobby watched them. He could tell that something terrible was happening between his parents, and he escaped as soon as he could to his own room. Johnny hadn't been around all afternoon, and he was out that evening. There was no one for Alice to talk to, and Jim took refuge in front of the TV, but without the familiar six-pack this time, much to his wife's amazement. She wished Johnny were there to say something to, but he didn't appear again until eleven that night, and by then, Jim had gone up to bed without a word, and Alice had stayed downstairs for a cup of tea.

"Where have you been?" she asked as though he'd been out on a date and missed his curfew. She forgot sometimes that she no longer had to worry about him. The worst had already happened.

"I had dinner with Buzz and Becky. He took her to a real cute place. He takes her to much nicer restaurants than

I did," he said with a grin, and she laughed at the absurdity of the situation. Just sitting at the kitchen table with him lightened her mood, and the anger that had pervaded the house since the night before.

"Are you supposed to just hang around with them like that?" she asked with a look of amusement. At least he didn't look upset by it. He seemed pleased for her, instead of jealous.

"No one said I couldn't. She sure talks about me a lot, Mom."

"I know she does," Alice said quietly. "She really loved you." She still did, Alice knew, but she didn't want to say that to him. There was no point reminding him, especially since he seemed in such good spirits after tagging along on Becky's date.

"They had a good time," Johnny said. "He's nice to her. He's trying to talk her into trying to get a scholarship at UCLA, so she can go back to school with him. She said she was going to try, but she doesn't think she'll get in. It would be great for her if she did." Alice nodded, watching him, and then he turned to her with a worried expression. "How was Dad tonight? Did you two make up?"

"Not really. He came home late again. But at least he was sober." She could be open about it with him. He was old enough to understand the tensions between them. But nonetheless she didn't tell him that she was wondering if he'd gone to the office at all, or was cheating on her.

"Give him a break, Mom," Johnny pleaded with her. "He's as upset about it as you are. He just doesn't know what to do."

"He needs to go to AA," she said, sounding angry and bitter.

"Maybe he will. Maybe the accident woke him up."

"He should have woken up five years ago, after Bobby's accident. It's getting to be a little late now." She sounded angry and bitter, and Johnny looked sad.

"Don't be so hard on him, Mom."

And just as he said that to her, the door opened and his father walked into the room. Alice had her mouth open and was about to say something else to Johnny when she saw him and stopped in midsentence. She thought he was asleep, but he had come back downstairs for something to eat.

"Talking to yourself again?" he asked, looking tired. She seemed to be doing that a lot lately. He could often hear it from the next room. "You ought to see a doctor about that," he said, as he left the kitchen and went back upstairs, and a few minutes later, Alice kissed Johnny good night, and followed suit.

They were in bed, side by side, before they spoke to each other again, "How's Charlotte feeling tonight?" He looked worried as he asked her.

"She's been asleep since this afternoon. You could go into her room in the morning and ask her yourself." But he had hidden from her all day. He was too embarrassed over what had happened to want to talk to her. He had apologized to her the night before, all the way home from the hospital, and she had reassured him that she was all right. But knowing the risk he'd taken had upset him more than her. She didn't want to make things any worse than they already were at home, and she had thanked him again for coming to her game, and taking her out, which made him feel even guiltier than ever.

"I'll talk to her tomorrow," he said vaguely, as he turned off the light, and lay next to Alice for a long time, wide awake, and thinking about his life.

Alice was already sound asleep when he finally curled up next to her, and fell into a deep sleep until morning. And when he stopped in to see Charlotte, she was still sleeping. Alice had gone to church, and Bobby was sitting alone in the kitchen. He had been talking to Johnny, but fell silent the moment he heard his father's footsteps approach.

Jim said nothing to him, poured himself a cup of coffee, and picked up the paper, as though Bobby weren't even in the room with him. And Johnny sat silent, watching. Johnny was still at the table with them, and he looked extremely pensive, as though he were concentrating on something. And after their father finished the paper, he put it down, and looked at Bobby, as though he'd suddenly had an idea.

"Your mom'll be back soon," he said, as though to a lost child who had wandered into their kitchen, a total stranger. He had no idea how to talk to him anymore. Since Bobby couldn't answer, to Jim, there seemed to be no point talking to him, and Bobby knew that. There were things Bobby would have liked to say to him, but knew he couldn't. And even now that he had begun speaking to Johnny and his mom again, he knew his father wouldn't understand. "Do you want something to eat?" Jim asked, not sure what the serious expression in the child's eyes meant, but he looked as though, for once, he was trying to understand. "Have you had breakfast?" Bobby nodded his head as Jim sighed.

"It's not easy talking to you," Jim said, not suffering from a hangover for the first time in years. He hadn't had a drink in nearly two days. "Why don't you answer, or at least try to? Don't you think you could talk, if you wanted to? I'll bet you could." He was wishing the child to talk to him, but there was not a sound from him. "You don't even try," he said, looking frustrated as Johnny gently touched his brother's hand, as though to reassure him that everything would be all right. He didn't need to be afraid of his father. Johnny wanted to convey to his brother that everything was going to be fine.

Jim stood up then, and there were tears in his eyes, as he walked out of the room. Their lives were falling apart. And Bobby sat in the kitchen for a long time, and then went upstairs quietly, and let himself into Johnny's room. He stayed in there for a long time, with Johnny, whispering, and looking at his trophies. And then he dropped something, and a moment later, his father opened the door to Johnny's room and saw Bobby there.

"What are you doing in here? You have no business coming in here. Go back to your room," he said sternly as tears filled Bobby's eyes, and Johnny whispered to him that he'd go with him, and not to let Dad scare him. It was going to be all right. The problem was that Johnny's room had finally become like a shrine in Jim's mind, and he didn't want any of Johnny's things disturbed, or removed.

Bobby walked silently out of the room, and when he'd gone, Jim walked slowly into the room. It was clean, everything was in order. Alice dusted it thoroughly once a week, and Jim didn't come in often enough to notice that things had been moved recently. Johnny had been spending a lot of time in his room, and going through his belongings and papers. There were photographs of him and Becky, letters, diaries he had kept as a kid. It was all still there, just as it had been when he left. And after a few minutes, Jim sat down on the bed, as tears streamed down his cheeks, and he looked around. It was five months since he'd been gone, and it was so painful seeing it just as it had once been. Johnny's varsity jacket was hanging over a chair, where he'd left it after he'd worn it the day before. Jim sat there for a long time, and then finally got up and left, and gently closed the door, and as he did, he saw Alice coming up the stairs. She knew where he had been, but said nothing.

She walked right past him into Charlotte's room, to check on her. She had just woken up, and said she was hungry and felt better. She went downstairs to eat breakfast in an old pink bathrobe, and smiled when she saw her father. She was still basking in the glow of his excitement about her game. The concussion she got afterward was far less important to her.

"How're you feeling, Charlie?" he asked, sounding hoarse from the tears he had just shed.

"Better. How 'bout you, Dad?" There was a new light in her eyes as she looked at him. She had shared her victory with him.

"I'm okay." Except that Alice had barely spoken to him in two days. Bobby looked at him like a stranger. And his hands had been shaking for two days since his last drink.

They all kept to themselves for the rest of the day, and at four o'clock, Jim went out. He came back two hours later, and didn't say anything to Alice about where he'd been. And she worried that he'd gone off to see some woman, as she thought he had the day before. But she made no comment when he came back, in better spirits, and she watched to see if he'd grab a six-pack. But he didn't. And instead of collapsing in front of the TV, he went outside to clean up the backyard. At dinner that night, he made feeble attempts to talk to her. Charlotte came downstairs and joined them, and she was already talking about going back to basketball practice the following week.

"Not until the doctor says you can," Alice scolded, and by the end of the meal, Jim was deep in conversation with his daughter about her style, and how good her game had been two days before.

"Thanks, Dad," she said, looking pleased. She had been told that more than likely she was going to be named most valuable player on her team at the last game. "Will you come to my game next week?"

"I'll try," he said with a cautious smile, first at his daughter, then his wife. But Bobby still seemed not to exist for him. His frustration at not being able to communicate with Bobby that morning had discouraged him.

Father and daughter went off to the living room after that, and Alice and the two boys stayed in the kitchen to clean up. The threesome were talking softly, but Charlotte could still hear her mother from the other room.

"She talks to herself all the time now," Charlotte confided to Jim, looking worried. Like her mother, she had noticed that her father wasn't drinking again that night, but she didn't comment on it.

"I think she talks to Bobby," he said with a sigh. "I don't know how she can. It's hard talking to someone who can't answer. I don't know what to say to him," he confided to her, and she felt a pang of sympathy for him.

"Bobby lets you know what he's thinking, if you pay attention to him," Charlotte said quietly. It was odd, but she felt as though she were making a connection with her father, for the first time in her life. She actually believed he liked and approved of her now that he'd watched her play.

"Do you suppose he'll ever talk

again?" It was odd asking her, but she seemed unusually wise to him now, for her fourteen years.

"Mom thinks he will one day. She says it takes time." Five years. And how much more? Jim thought to himself. "Johnny used to talk to him a lot. You should shoot some baskets with him sometime, Dad."

"Does he like that?" Jim looked surprised. He had no idea what his youngest son did and didn't like, and never tried to find out.

She nodded. "He's pretty good for a kid."

"So are you," he smiled, and then he put an arm around her as they sat on the couch. He turned the television on after a while, and they watched a football game. And a little later, Bobby came and sat next to them. Johnny was in a chair, sprawled out and enjoying the scene with his siblings, and from time to time Bobby smiled at him. It was as though having Johnny there encouraged him to try his wings.

And when Alice emerged from the kitchen, and looked at them, she smiled too. In spite of her anger at her husband, she had to admit that things seemed to have improved. Ever since his accident with Charlotte, Jim had stopped drinking. It hadn't gone unnoticed, and she was afraid to mention it to him. But she was well aware that he hadn't had a drink since. And the atmosphere of the whole house seemed to have changed. She was thinking about it that night when she went upstairs to their room, and again the next day when she dropped Bobby off at school.

She was singing to herself and doing some sewing when the phone rang, and she wondered if it was Jim. He was usually the only person who called her during the day. Everyone else she knew was working. But he hadn't called her in months. Ever since Johnny died, he had been shut off from everyone, and feeling isolated, even from her.

But when she answered the phone, it wasn't Jim, but Bobby's school. He had fallen off the swing at school, and broken his wrist. The teacher was at the emergency room with him, and she said she'd be bringing him home soon. Alice was upset they hadn't called her sooner, but the teacher said they hadn't had time before they went to the hospital, and it distressed Alice not to have been with him at the hospital. But he came home ten minutes later, with a slightly groggy look. They had given him medicine for the pain. And she put him on his bed, and left him with Johnny, while the teacher waited for her.

"The doctor at the emergency room said he'd be fine soon. He has to keep the cast on for four weeks." She seemed to hesitate then, and looked as though she had something else to say. "I don't want to get your hopes up, and I could be wrong," the teacher ventured slowly into unfamiliar waters with her, "but I thought I heard him say 'ow' when he fell." Had Alice not known that he'd started talking, she would have been ecstatic, but now she just looked pensive, and told the teacher she might have misheard him. She said she had often imagined him speaking simply because she wished he would. She was not yet ready to share with the world the fact that he could speak. She wanted to protect him for as long as she could, until he was completely confident again.

"I could have imagined it." The teacher nodded. "But I don't think I did." Johnny had been insistent that Bobby go slow, and that they not tell anyone yet. And Alice wanted Jim to know before they told the world. "Maybe you should have him tested again," the teacher suggested, and Alice thanked her, and offered the woman a cup of tea before she left.

Alice had both children at home now, Charlotte with her concussion and Bobby with his broken wrist, and when Jim came home that night, late as usual, he made a fuss over both of them. He still wasn't drinking, and finally, when the kids went upstairs, Alice looked at him.

"Where have you been going after work these days?" she asked with eyes filled with suspicion. He seemed healthier, in better spirits, and more sober than he had been in years. But he was coming home later than usual every night.

"Nowhere," he said vaguely, and then he saw in her eyes everything she feared, and he felt sorry for her. "I've just been going to some meetings after work."

"What kind of meetings?" she asked, looking for clues in his eyes, and he didn't answer her for a long time. But finally his eyes met hers more honestly than they had in a long time.

"Does it matter?"

"It does to me. A lot. Are you seeing someone else?" Her breath caught as she asked the question.

He reached out and touched her hand as he shook his head. "I wouldn't do that to you, Alice. I love you. I'm sorry everything has gotten so screwed up . . . with Johnny . . . and Bobby's accident . . . and now Charlotte getting hurt. . . . Things sure got messed up here. And no, I'm not seeing another woman. I've been going to AA meetings. I got it, after hitting that truck the other night. It was time to stop drinking."

As she looked at him, Alice's eyes filled with tears, and he leaned over and kissed her. It was a dream come true.

"Thank you" was all she could say. And when they went to their room that night, they locked the door when they went to bed, so the children wouldn't disturb them. Johnny was nowhere in sight, and was asleep, curled up on the foot of Bobby's bed.

Chapter Ten

December was a busy month for all of them. Jim's business was taking off. He had three new clients in addition to the two he'd gotten a few months before, and his workload seemed to have increased tenfold. Alice wasn't sure if his giving up drinking had anything to do with it, but he seemed to be working harder, and earning more. And he was more relaxed than he had been in years. He was even taking some afternoons off, or leaving work early at least, to go to some of Charlotte's games. He had become her chief adviser on what he was convinced was a promising athletic career. And now he bragged about her at least as much as, if not more than, he had about Johnny.

Charlotte was basking in the warmth of it. She had just turned fifteen, and the local paper had run her photograph on the sports page. Boys were suddenly of more interest to her, and there was one in particular she liked on a local boys' team. But it was her father's company and approval she craved these days, as though she were making up for all the lost years when he had virtually ignored her. He had talked about it in his AA meetings, and even made amends to her in his Ninth Step, and Charlotte had been startled when he cried when he apologized. He had explained that it had never dawned on him that she could be the fine athlete she was, even though she was a girl. But even if she hadn't been, he would have loved her. He had just been numb for so long that he had lost her. He apologized for all the times he had dismissed her, ignored her, and celebrated Johnny's accomplishments, and never hers. His apology led to a bond between them stronger than any they'd ever had before. And when he was making amends to her, he wished that he could have made amends to Bobby too. But he still felt strange talking to him, and just looking at the child brought back waves of guilt over the accident they'd had because he had been drinking at the time.

Alice was enjoying watching the relationship develop between Charlotte and Jim. She and Johnny talked about it, and the miracle that had come into their life when Jim joined AA. Alice knew without asking him that Johnny had prodded him to it, just as he had opened his father's heart to Charlotte after all these years.

"That was quite an accomplishment," she said to Johnny while he was helping her do laundry one day. "A miracle actually. Two miracles." He had stopped drinking, and he had come to love and appreciate Charlotte in all the ways he never had.

And Bobby speaking again was another miracle Johnny could take credit for, although Bobby still wouldn't speak to anyone but Johnny and his mother. But Johnny said that when he was ready to, he would. He thought he should get more sure of himself first. But that moment seemed to be approaching daily. He smiled a lot more now, ventured out of his room more frequently, seemed more present in the family, and was doing really well in school. And when he was with Johnny and his mother, he chattered constantly, and seemed to have a million things to say, and stories to tell.

"What about you, Mom?" Johnny asked her as she started an apple pie for dinner that night. "What do you really want?" She never seemed to ask for anything.

"You," she said, as she turned to him. "I wish you could come back for good." But they both knew that was impossible, and he would have if he could. "I'm so glad you've been here for a while."

He had been back for two months, but
as Alice looked around at her family, she
saw that he was accomplishing all the
miracles for which he had come, and in-
evitably it worried her. Once his work
was done, he would have to leave them
again. They had never talked about it,
but she sensed now that his work here
was almost finished. "You won't just
disappear, will you?" she asked, with
worried eyes, as she rolled out the crust
for the pie she was baking for dinner.

"No, Mom. You'll know," he said
quietly. "I wouldn't do that to you." It
had been hard enough surviving the
shock and suddenness when he died.
She couldn't bear the thought of going
through that again. "You'll be ready this
time," he said, reading her mind, and
answering her.

"I'll never be ready for you to go,"
she said stubbornly, with tears in her
eyes. "I wish you could stay here, just
like this, forever."

"You know I would if I could,
Mom," Johnny said, coming to put an

arm around her. "But I promise, you'll be ready by the time I have to go. It won't ever be like last time." The memory of it, the sheer horror and agony of losing him, made her shudder, remembering those first days.

"We're lucky we've had the last two months with you," she said softly, trying to remind herself to count her blessings. "Have you already done everything you came to do here?"

"I don't think so," he said, sounding a little uncertain. It had never been absolutely clear to him what he had come for, but as things unfolded, it was easy to see all the good he'd been doing. And he himself had a sense that one by one he was accomplishing the appointed tasks. His assignment had never been spelled out to him. But he could sense what was needed day by day. "I think we'll both know when that happens." But they both had a sense that it wasn't far away. Watching him she had become more intuitive too.

"And will you just vanish into thin air

then?" she asked him with a look of panic.

"I told you, Mom," he said, looking far beyond his years suddenly, "I won't do that to you. They wouldn't expect it of me." He had been sent to heal, not to hurt.

"Good," she said, sounding relieved, "it would be nice to have some warning."

"I think when the time comes, we'll both know." But she was already getting that feeling, even if he wasn't. Jim had stopped drinking after years of alcoholism, he and Charlotte had bonded as never before, he was an integral part now of her athletic activities, and went to every game he could get to. And Bobby was talking, even if only in secret. "I think I still have some fine-tuning to do here."

"Well, don't rush anything," she said with a grin, and he laughed at her. "Maybe you could drag your feet just a little bit."

"I'll go real slow, Mom. I promise."

"I love you," she whispered into his neck as he hugged her. And that afternoon he went to see Becky. Things were going well at her house too.

She had been seeing a lot of Buzz, and she seemed very happy whenever Alice saw her. She no longer looked as devastated as she had in the months before. She laughed a lot more now, and she seemed more relaxed, just as Pam did. Her romance with Gavin had blossomed over the holidays, and he was talking about moving, to be closer to her.

Alice was trimming the tree with Johnny late one afternoon, playing CDs of Christmas carols and singing with him, when Jim came home from work early. He had forgotten some papers at home, and decided to work on them there, and he smiled when he saw Alice trimming the Christmas tree, and heard her singing.

"How did you manage the star on the top all by yourself this year?" It was a tough one to explain to him, and she just said that when the mailman came, he helped her. And Jim seemed satisfied with the story. Johnny chuckled as he listened to her and smiled broadly. He had put all the decorations on the top branches for her, as he always had.

"That was creative," Johnny teased her, and she laughed, and then said something to him when she thought Jim wasn't listening, but when he came back into the living room again, he was frowning.

"We're going to have to do something about your talking to yourself. Maybe you should go to 'Talking-to-yourself Anonymous,'" he teased. "Charlotte worries about you. She thinks it's because of Johnny."

"I guess it is, sort of. I'll get over it." All too soon, she feared. When Johnny left again, there would be no one to talk to. Not like that anyway. There was Jim, of course, and the children. But her oldest child had always been her soul mate, and still was. More than ever now. "I guess it's just become a habit," she said to her husband, as he disappeared again with his briefcase and a stack of papers.

He was still working on them when Charlotte came home from school, and Alice went to pick up Bobby, and took Johnny with her. They chatted easily all the way to Bobby's school, and he laughed at what his father had said about her talking to him.

"By the time you leave, everyone will be convinced I'm crazy," his mother complained with a rueful smile.

"That's not such a bad thing," Johnny said, lying across the backseat, and hanging his feet out the window. He was a lot taller than his father. "You can do anything you want then. 'Crazy Mrs. Peterson.' It could be very liberating, Mom. It sounds like fun."

"Not to me. I don't want people thinking I'm loony." But it was a good kind of "crazy," and such a good feeling being with him, a constant blend of seriousness and laughter and joy.

In the last few months, Johnny had developed even greater insight and astonishing wisdom about people and sensitive situations. He understood his father better than he ever had, and he seemed to sense Bobby's feelings and needs without even trying. He could see right into Charlotte's heart, and know everything she thought and worried about. And he was closer than ever to his mother. Sometimes they each knew what the other was thinking, without even talking. They always had been able to do that, but it was even stronger now. Theirs was a tie that defied what had happened to them, and could never be severed. And she knew that even when he left again, she would never lose him now. It was comforting knowing that, and they both smiled in precisely the same way as Bobby came bounding out of school with a box of handmade Christmas decorations he'd made in art class.

"Perfect timing!" she said as she kissed her youngest child, and he piled into the backseat with Johnny. "Johnny and I decorated the tree today."

"How does it look?" Bobby asked, beaming at them.

"Pretty good. But it'll look better now with all your beautiful decorations." She smiled lovingly at him. He was as precious to her as Johnny was, he was just different. And she adored Charlotte too. But Johnny was part of her soul forevermore.

"Do you like 'em, Mom?" Bobby asked, holding up his favorites to her.

"Yes, I do, sweetheart. We'll put them on the tree the minute we get home." It was still another two weeks until Christmas. And everyone in the family had a lot to do. Jim was organizing an office Christmas party, and had a lot of year-end tax work to do for his many clients. Charlotte was wrapping up her basketball season, and was in the play-offs and an all-star game that she and her father were really looking forward to. And Bobby was going to be an angel in his school play. All he had to do was flap his wings and walk across the stage several times. He didn't have a speaking part, for obvious reasons, but he was very much a part of it anyway. And Alice had made his costume, and finished it that week.

She and Jim weren't giving a party this year, but they had invited the Adamses to join them on Christmas Eve. Pam was bringing Gavin too. He was planning to take a week off and spend the holidays with her and the children.

And when they actually appeared on Christmas Eve, everyone was in high spirits. Alice had made homemade eggnog for them, with alcohol in theirs, and none in Jim's. And he was so jovial that Pam said she hardly recognized him. He and Gavin hit it off immediately, and within minutes, Jim was bragging about Charlotte just the way he once had about Johnny. Alice couldn't help but think of it, as she listened to him. It was just what Charlotte had always longed for, and wanted from him. For her, life had improved immeasurably since the first game her father had finally come to.

The only one who still seemed left out was Bobby. Jim still could not bring himself to deal with him easily. And Bobby only came to life when he was alone with his mother and Johnny, and chattering away with them a mile a minute, as though to make up for lost time.

Becky looked particularly pretty that night in a black velvet dress and high heels that Gavin had bought for her. He was extremely generous with Pam, and took great pleasure in helping her with the children. He enjoyed buying things for them, and doing things with them. With no children of his own, they were the instant family he had always dreamed of and never had.

He and Pam waited until after dinner to make an announcement. Gavin had just raised his glass to all of them, Adamses and Petersons alike, and he wished them all a beautiful Christmas, as Becky's youngest brother guffawed and said that was really corny. But he said it in a good-natured way that indicated they were good friends. All of the Adams children really liked him. And so did Pam. She loved him. Maybe not as much as she'd loved Mike after so many years and five kids, but more than enough to want to share her life with him. They told the assembled company over coffee and dessert that they were getting married in June.

They wanted some time to find a house, and he had offered to put the kids in better schools and pay for it. He wanted the very best for them, and for Pam, or the best he could do for them at least. He was a very generous person. And all of the Petersons congratulated them, as Alice noticed out of the corner of her eye that Johnny was sitting on the floor, near the Christmas tree, and watching them. As usual, he couldn't keep his eyes off Becky. She looked lovelier than ever, and like her old self again, although there was a nostalgic look in her eye each time she talked about the things she had done with Johnny. But she was still very young and had a lifetime ahead of her. Johnny knew it, and sensed that she would be happy now without him.

"What about you?" Alice asked Becky. "You're not getting married, are you?" She was only half-teasing.

"I should hope not! She's too young!" Johnny shouted from the living room, and Bobby burst out laughing. The others looked at him, surprised, and he immediately fell back into silence, while Alice shot him a warning look, and a few minutes later, stepped into the living room to scold Johnny.

"Have you gotten into the eggnog? What are you doing shouting like that?"

"No one can hear me, Mom, except you and Bobby. I can shout all I want, and sing, and do cartwheels," he said, demonstrating one for her, and nearly crashing into the coffee table.

"I think you need some exercise or something."

"I'm just having fun," he smiled at her as she shook her head and went back to the others. Johnny was doing push-ups next to the Christmas tree when she left him, and singing as loud as he could.

"What were you doing in there?" Jim asked gently. Pam had commented while she was gone that she was still talking to herself a lot of the time. And Charlotte said she always did now, when she was in the kitchen alone or in their bedroom before Jim came up at night. She sounded just like she was talking to a friend or something. "I think she imagines she's talking to your brother," he said softly, but even more than the others, he worried about her. She seemed so well balanced and sane, but it was obvious to all of them that she hadn't recovered from her son's death, and maybe never would, particularly not if she was "talking" to him. It was particularly poignant as it was their first Christmas without him.

"I was just making sure the Christmas tree lights were on," Alice said, looking unconcerned, when Jim asked her what she'd been doing. It sounded like a rea-

sonable explanation, but didn't explain
the whispered conversation that Jim had
heard when he stood in the doorway
and listened to her. He just hoped she'd
get over it eventually, and regain her
balance again. He was feeling closer to
her than he had in a long time.

They talked about Pam and Gavin's
wedding after that, and all their plans.
They knew exactly what kind of house
they wanted. And once they found it,
and got it ready for themselves, they
were going to put Pam's house and his
in L.A. on the market. The children said
they'd be sad to leave their old house,
but they were excited about everything
Gavin had said to them. He had even
promised to buy a boat to use on the
lake next summer.

And then Pam turned to Becky, and
told her to share her news with them.
She blushed for a minute, and Johnny
panicked as he watched her. He had
come back to the table to sit in one of
the chairs Becky's siblings had vacated.
They had all gone upstairs with Bobby

and Charlotte, to watch videos in Charlotte's bedroom.

"She's not getting married, is she, Mom?" he asked with a terrified expression, not that he could stop her now, or even wanted to, but in some ways, he still hated her being with someone else, and he knew he had to get over it. He wanted her happiness, but he still felt a pang when he thought of bowing out of her life. He had introduced Buzz to her, and he didn't begrudge her her happiness, and yet all he wanted when he looked at her was to put his arms around her one last time. But since she couldn't see him, he couldn't. He held her hand sometimes, but she had no sense of it. The only people he could hug and kiss and touch were Bobby and his mother. And he couldn't help wondering what would have happened if Becky had been able to see him the way they did. Maybe that was why that hadn't been allowed to happen. If it had, it would have been even harder for him to leave when the time came.

"What's your news, Becky?" Alice prodded. Johnny looked as though he were about to explode as he waited.

"I got a scholarship," she said, sounding very modest about it. "At UCLA. I'm starting in January. And Buzz is going back to school then too. He really helped me get it," she said, looking very happy.

"No, he didn't," Johnny said petulantly, as his mother looked at him, "I did." Alice nodded, as though agreeing with him, but she couldn't say anything with all the others watching her.

"That's wonderful, dear," she said, knowing how proud Pam must be of her. She had gotten a full scholarship, and was planning to be an art major. Alice had collected at least a dozen sketches of Johnny from her over the years, and she was very good. She said she wanted to take art history classes too, and be an art teacher when she graduated. Johnny had always thought it would be a great career for her. And she was on her way now.

After dinner, Pam went out to the kitchen to help Alice clean up, and the two men went into the living room to discuss business, and taxes, politics, and sports, while Johnny sat with them. It wasn't a conversation that interested him much, but he was afraid he would make his mother seem odd if he went out to the kitchen with her, and made too many comments to her that she would be tempted to respond to. It seemed better to stay away from her, so he sat in a chair and listened to his father and Gavin talk, and then he saw Becky going upstairs to join the others, and instinctively he followed her. But she didn't turn toward Charlotte's room, where the others were watching videos. Instead, she walked soundlessly to Johnny's room, opened the door, and slipped quietly inside before anyone could notice. She shut the door behind her, and stood there for a long moment, breathing in his familiar smell, and she lay down on his bed in the moonlight and closed her eyes. He was standing right next to her, and he gently touched her hand, but she couldn't feel it, except in her heart. She could feel his presence in the room with her, and a strange peace seemed to fill her.

She knew his room so well, and him, and his life, all his dreams, and the things he had once hoped for, all the secrets they'd shared with each other.

"I love you, Johnny," she whispered, and closed her eyes, as he looked at her.

"I love you too, Becky. I always will." And then as though a force greater than him made him say it, "I want you to be happy. You're going to have a great time in college . . . and if you want to be with Buzz, and he makes you happy," he nearly choked on the words but knew he had to say them anyway, "I just want you to have a good life, with him, or someone else. You deserve it, Becky. You know I'll always love you." She nodded, as though she could hear him, in her head, in her heart, in the dreams they had once shared. She felt peaceful and warm, and after a long time, she got up, and wandered around the room, touching his photographs and treasures and trophies. She stood for a long time, looking at her favorite photograph of him. She had the same one next to her bed at home, but there was one of Buzz there now too. But as she looked at Johnny's picture now, it was as though she could really see him.

"I'll always love you, Johnny," she whispered, and there were tears in his eyes when he answered her.

"I will too, Becky. Have a great life now," he told her, and meant it, and she nodded and then wandered to the door of the room, and stood there for a long time. And then, without another word, she left the room, and closed the door silently behind her. She had a sense of peace and freedom and joy that she hadn't had since he died, and when she went to find the others in Charlotte's room, she was smiling as she wiped her eyes. In an odd way, she felt as though she had just said good-bye to Johnny, in a way she could live with. Not with the wrenching agony of six months before, but with a sense of love and peace and letting go. She knew that she would always take him with her now. But she was ready to move on.

The Adamses left at eleven-thirty, just as the Petersons were getting ready to go to midnight mass, and they all hugged and kissed and wished each other a Merry Christmas. The Adams troop drove off in the van Gavin had bought to chauffeur them, and the Petersons waved as they drove off. There were only four of them now. To Charlotte and Jim, it was so obvious that someone was missing. But Johnny was sitting between Charlie and Bobby in the backseat, as his parents chatted, and Jim put on a tape of Christmas carols. In a way, the holidays were painful for all of them this year, but they had to count their blessings too, and lately there had been a lot of them.

Jim dozed through part of the service, and Charlotte fidgeted, as Alice closed her eyes and listened to the music.

Every now and then she opened them, and smiled at Bobby and Johnny and Charlie. They were her real Christmas gifts, as Jim was now. She had never been happier with them.

The only thing that marred the day for her was that on the way home she complained to Jim that she had indigestion.

"It's not your ulcer again?" he asked, looking worried. She had been so desperately sick in October that he had nearly lost her, and the memory of that filled him with terror now, but she was quick to reassure him.

"I just ate too much turkey," she said easily, and Pam's mince pie had been a little heavy. But she forgot about it as they got back to the house, and she started to usher Bobby up to bed. He was wide awake, and he hesitated as she took his hand, and he looked up at her, as though to ask her a question. And she wasn't entirely sure what he meant by it. He just stood there, staring at her, and then at his father, and suddenly she wondered. She looked over at Johnny and he was smiling as he nodded at Bobby. And suddenly Alice understood, as tears filled her eyes, and she looked tenderly at her husband. "I think Bobby has something to say to you," she said as Jim and Charlotte watched him. Bobby's eyes never left his father's. It was as though it was something he owed him, and had for a long time, and now he was going to give it to him. It was the Christmas gift that would mean more to Jim than any other for the rest of his life.

"Merry Christmas, Dad," Bobby said softly, as Jim stared at him and then choked on a sob, as he reached his arms out to him, and held him tight, as the others watched them.

"What happened to you?" Jim asked hoarsely. "How did this happen?" He looked from his son to his wife, as Charlotte cried, and Johnny smiled benevolently on them. He was so proud of all of them, his brother, his dad, Charlie for all she'd done and accomplished, and his mom for all she had endured and believed in, and given.

"I just started talking to . . ." Bobby caught his mother's eye, which warned him to be careful, and not give away their secret, ". . . to myself. . . . I've been practicing since Thanksgiving."

"And you waited all this time to tell me?"

"I had to," Bobby said with a smile, "you weren't ready." Jim pondered the meaning of his words for a moment, and then nodded agreement.

"Maybe I wasn't. But I am now." It was as though the last five painfully silent years had vanished in a single moment.

"I love you, Dad," Bobby whispered as his father held him.

"I love you too, son," Jim said, taking his hand, and the two walked up the stairs, hand in hand, and Alice watched them, feeling the true wonder of Christmas.

Chapter Eleven

On Christmas morning, Bobby came thundering down the stairs to find his presents under the tree, and a few minutes later, Charlotte and his parents joined them. Jim had bought Charlotte all kinds of sports equipment that she had wanted, including an automatic ball machine, so she could practice hitting that spring. It was something he knew she longed for.

And he had bought Alice a sweater set, a new coat, and a gold bracelet. And she loved all of it. She had given him a beautiful new leather briefcase, and a suede jacket he had seen and wanted. And he loved it.

Bobby got a small mountain of toys

that Johnny had helped their mother pick out for him, and he loved every one of them, and was happily putting together parts, and inserting batteries to make them work five minutes later. Their gifts were all a big success. And it was only when she was cooking breakfast for all of them, the banana waffles they ate every year on Christmas morning, that Alice felt sick again. She knew it was from excitement and the nagging worry now that Johnny would soon be going. But she tried not to think of it as she served them the breakfast they loved every year. And when she turned to look at him, she noticed that Johnny was looking tired. He had done so much work for all of them that it had exhausted him, but he seemed to be in good spirits, when he stood over her, practically drooling for her waffles.

"I sure wish I could eat them, Mom," he said, looking like a kid again, and Alice smiled at him, wishing he could too. She wished a lot of things, that he had never died, that he could stay here

now, that she could hold on to him forever, but she knew she couldn't. And it
wouldn't have been fair to him. He had
to go on, to do what he was meant to.
It was his destiny. But it didn't seem fair
to her that he had died, that he had been
so young when he left them.

Jim and Charlotte had second help-
ings of the waffles, while Bobby chattered constantly, explaining his new toys
to them, how they worked, and how to
assemble them, as his father smiled
broadly.

"He's sure making up for lost time,
isn't he?" Jim said after their children
left the kitchen, except for Johnny, who
was still sitting at the kitchen table, enjoying the dizzying aroma of his
mother's waffles. She hadn't eaten any
this year, she had just picked at them,
but none of them had noticed. Except
Johnny. "Why do you suppose he
started talking again?" Jim asked, as he
looked admiringly at her. Alice had
never looked more beautiful to him, as
he leaned over and kissed her. "What do

you suppose did it?" he persisted about Bobby. For him, it was like the ultimate absolution. Bobby had paid for five years for his father's stupidity, and now he was free of what had seemed to Jim like a curse on all of them. It was the most perfect blessing.

"I think a miracle did it," Alice said simply, and Jim didn't disagree with her. He was just grateful it had happened.

He went to watch a football game then, and Charlotte joined him, as Alice puttered around the kitchen, and eventually Bobby went to sit with them, dragging half his toys with him.

"Are you okay, Mom?" Johnny asked her, looking worried.

"I'm fine," she said more out of habit than truth. She wasn't feeling terrific, but she didn't want to worry him. She knew it was her stomach again, and she hated the thought that she might be getting another ulcer. But she had no intention of saying that and ruining Christmas for him, or the others. "Honest, it's nothing."

"I'm not as sure of that as you are," Johnny said, sounding very grown up. "You'd better go to the doctor tomorrow."

"I will if it still bothers me," she promised.

They spent a lazy afternoon, eating and watching TV, and that night, she cooked the traditional ham that she always made for them at Christmas. Her appetite wasn't great, and she was distracted as she served the dinner. But all afternoon, she had been haunted by the realization that the miracles they'd experienced and the blessings they'd shared had been too numerous. There was nothing left for Johnny to do now. Becky had her scholarship and a new boyfriend who was good to her. Pam had met a wonderful man, who loved her, and her kids, and they were getting married. Charlotte and Jim were closer than anyone could ever have dreamed of. He had stopped drinking. Bobby had started talking. And she had had nearly three months with the son she loved and who had been taken from her, with no warning, all too quickly. They had each had priceless gifts that would change the course of their lives forever. There was nothing left to do. And the more she thought of it, the more she knew that Johnny would have to leave soon. And the prospect of it made her heart ache.

"You're leaving, aren't you?" she asked him when they were alone in the kitchen after dinner. Everything was put away, and it had been a long, comfortable day. Even Johnny's absence hadn't been as painful as usual, for Jim and Charlotte. They seemed to be adjusting to it, and Johnny had explained to Bobby, right from the beginning, that he would leave again one day. He was just there for a little visit.

"Probably, Mom," Johnny said honestly. "We'll know when it's the right time. You will too. I told you, you'll be ready." He sounded so certain of it, but she hadn't liked his answer.

"Then it's not the right time," she

said, sounding younger than he did, "because I'm *not* ready. This is going to hurt too much," she said, as tears spilled onto her cheeks, and Johnny looked at her sadly.

"Don't cry, Mom. I won't be far away. You know that."

"I want you here, just like you have been."

"I know you do. So do I. We all do. But I can't do that. They won't let me. I have to go back." His stay for the past several months had been the ultimate gift.

"That's mean of them," she said, as he put his arms around her. "We need you . . . I need you . . . and Bobby and Dad, and Charlie."

"I love you," he said simply, and for an instant, she got a glimmer of what that meant. The words seemed enormous suddenly, like the feelings that went with them. Bigger than she'd ever imagined they could be. The words were like clouds that enveloped her, and cushioned all the pain she'd ever felt, or been afraid of, since the beginning of time.

"You look tired," she said, looking up at him. "And you know I love you too."

"Yes, I do, Mom. I always knew that." She was relieved to hear it. They stood and hugged for a long moment, and then walked slowly out of the kitchen to find the others. Everyone was looking full and tired and sleepy. And a little while later, they all walked upstairs together, wished each other a Merry Christmas again, and went to their own rooms.

She and Jim went to bed early, and the kids were already asleep, as they lay there talking about what a nice Christmas it had been, despite the painful reality of Johnny's absence. And she felt a little guilty when Jim mentioned it, because only she and Bobby knew that Johnny had been there with them.

"You know, I feel good about him. As though he's in a happy place. I don't know why, but I just feel that," Jim said, as they lay in the dark, with his arm around her.

"So do I," she said with a sigh, and then they just lay side by side and held each other. And a little while later, Jim fell asleep, but Alice just couldn't. She was wide awake, no matter how tired she was, or how long the day had been. All she could think of tonight was Johnny. And long after midnight, she got up finally, and walked out into the hallway. She was going to go back downstairs and make herself a cup of warm milk to drink, to soothe her nerves and calm her stomach. And just as she came out of her room, she saw Johnny come out of Charlotte's bedroom. He had been with her for a long time, and held her hand as she fell asleep, and she was smiling now, dreaming of him.

He had been in Bobby's room with him before that, and they'd had a long talk, about what it meant to go on, and take the people you love with you in your heart.

"You're going away again, aren't you?" Bobby had asked him, but he hadn't looked worried about it. It was as though he understood, even though he was a child.

"Yes, I am." Johnny was always honest with him.

"Will you come back again?" Bobby's eyes were wide with wonder.

"Maybe, but I don't think so."

"Thank you for helping me talk again," Bobby said, and they held each other for a long time. Bobby would always remember his brother, and in many ways, he was a lot like him.

Johnny was telling his mother about it, as they started down the stairs, and then he stopped and went to his room, and looked around for a minute. He was going to miss all of them, he knew, as much as they missed him. And he reminded his mother to give Bobby his varsity jacket when he was big enough to wear it. And Charlotte could borrow it in the meantime. Tears sprang to her eyes the minute he said it. It was time

for good-byes again. And she had never
wanted to say good-bye to him the first
time, she had refused to. Maybe that was
why he had come back to them, because
she had refused to let him go. Or maybe
he had come back to attend to unfinished business. But he had finished all of
it. All the loose ends were tied up, so
neatly and so well, like everything he
had done in life. In three months, he
had done so much for so many people.
Alice couldn't help thinking how
blessed they had all been.

Johnny watched her warm the milk,
and then sat down with her, while she
drank it. And when she finished it, she
looked up at him. She knew now why
she hadn't been able to sleep that night.
He was going. She couldn't even bring
herself to say the words to him. The
idea of it was too painful, but he shook
his head as he looked at her.

"Don't do it that way, Mom. Let me
go this time. I'll be here with you, always, even when you can't see me."

"I'm going to miss talking to you.

What am I going to do without you?"
she asked, with tears in her eyes.

"You'll be busy, with Dad and the
others." He smiled at her and put his
arms around her, and after a while they
stood up, and she looked at him with
everything she felt for him, and had
since the day he was born.

"I love you, Johnny."

"I love you too, Mom . . . more than
you'll ever know . . . more than I ever
told you."

"You are such a good boy, and I'm so
proud of you . . . I always will be."

"I'm proud of you too." And then he
turned, as though he'd forgotten something, and he pulled a small rectangular
box out of his pocket. He had wrapped
it awkwardly, and he handed it to her.
"This is for you and Dad. It's going to
make you happy for a long, long time,
all your lives, I hope."

"What is it? Should I open it now?"
She was curious about what was in it.

"No, do it later," he said firmly, and

she slipped it into the pocket of her bathrobe.

And then he walked slowly to the door, and she followed him. They stood there for a long time, looking out into the night, and hugging. He had his arms around her and held her tight, just as he had as a child. She could feel the warm milk she had drunk warm her. She felt peaceful and tired, and strangely comfortable, and he held her for a long time, and then kissed her cheek. She kissed him one last time, and he walked out into the night, as she watched him. She wanted to stop him, or run after him, but she knew she couldn't. He turned back once to smile at her, and she was smiling at him as tears poured from her eyes, but it was a different kind of sadness this time, mixed with longing and joy and gratitude for all he had been to her. She blinked for only an instant to clear the tears from her eyes, and he was gone, walking softly into the night, to a place where she could not follow.

She stood in the doorway for a long time, and then closed it softly. It was hard to believe he was gone, impossible, as hard as it had been the first time. But he was right, it was different. She missed him already, and she was not sure she was as ready as he had said she would be. Her heart was full of him as she walked back upstairs to her bedroom. And as she looked at Jim, sleeping peacefully, she knew that Johnny would always be with them. And when she put the dressing gown down, she remembered the little gift Johnny had left them.

She walked into the bathroom and turned on the light, to open it. And when she did, she laughed out loud. It was a crazy gift. Just a joke, and nothing important. It was a pregnancy kit, the kind you bought in the drugstore, it was like a message from him, telling her to do something she and Jim hadn't thought about in years. They had thought about having a fourth child once upon a time, but after Bobby's ac-

cident, they had decided they couldn't.
And as she held the box in her hand, it
was as though she heard Johnny's voice
in her head, telling her to use it.

"Go on, Mom . . . go on . . . do
it. . . ." The words were so clear, it was
as though he were still standing there
with her, and she wondered if he was,
but she could no longer see him or hear
him. She could only feel him, in her
heart. The past three months had been a
crazy time, but a time she would always
cherish. And as she thought of it, she
suddenly thought of the ulcer she was so
convinced had returned in the past few
days, the disturbance she had felt, and
she wondered if Johnny really was
telling her something with his silly gift.
She couldn't imagine it happening, but
feeling foolish, she decided to follow the
impulse and use it.

And five minutes later, as she stood
holding the test and read the results, she
knew that the voice had been as clear as
though he had been standing with her.
He still was, always would be with her,

and his gift to her, his miracle, had not only been his visit. There was a new life in her, a new vista opening up to her. She could feel him next to her as she thought of it. One life had ended, and another was beginning. And Johnny, the boy she had loved so much and never lost, her son and soul mate, would always be in her heart with her.